Wilson Roberts

Lisa Long

Incident on Tuckerman Court

Fantastic Books
PO Box 243
Blacksburg VA 24063
www.fantasticbooks.wilderpublications.com

ISBN 10: 1-60459-996-0
ISBN 13: 978-1-60459-996-1

First Edition

Incident on Tuckerman Court
by Wilson Roberts

One

"I have accepted Christ, Tommy," my wife said. "Jesus entered my heart and told me to follow him the rest of my days."

I felt as though I had been stabbed in the heart.

Jan's revelation was spoken in a tone no different than that she might use to tell a patient her latest ultra-sound had confirmed the baby she was carrying was a boy, or she had a tumor in her fallopian tubes, as if the disclosure of an obstetrical or gynecological truth were no more unusual than her confession of spiritual revelation.

Sitting across the table, her morning coffee still steaming, she leaned toward me, the only sign of her emotional state an unusual wetness in her eyes, yet the message she had delivered was as life altering as the most devastating medical disclosure.

The comment seemed to have come out of nowhere. Jan and I had just gotten back the day before from a week in New York. We had gone to museums, wandered through Central Park, and eaten in sidewalk bistros pretending we were in Paris. The weather had been unusually warm and sunny for late March, and we explored the Morningside Heights area around the Upper West Side apartment we had borrowed from friends. The week had been filled with the laughter and easy companionship that can come with a long and successful marriage. There had been no hint that she would soon make such a drastic disclosure.

I had just finished reading an article on the Presidential primaries and, putting the paper down, I took a long sip of coffee and heaved a deep sigh.

"It's April 3rd, and I'm already sick of political punditry," I had said. "How are we going to make it to November?"

Instead of answering, she cleared her throat and told me Jesus had entered her heart. I didn't say anything for several long minutes, and she sat still, her eyes never leaving my face. I looked beyond her at two squirrels racing along the top of the fence separating our neighbor's paved-over yard from our half acre of gardens and fruit trees. I did not know how to respond. I would have been less shocked if she said she had fallen I love with one of her patients and was leaving me. She had always been the most rational of beings, a rock of sanity I relied upon.

The lead squirrel leapt from the fence to a lower limb on a nearby sugar maple, and in seconds it was near the tree top, chattering as the other squirrel leapt after it, and the two of them chased one another from tree to tree.

"You've become a Christian?"

"Being Christian implies a churchliness I'm not comfortable with. I do know that Jesus is with me, and with him in my heart I finally know true peace and comfort."

"And that's not being a Christian?"

"Not by any organized religious standards. I've had an individual experience with Jesus that bears no relationship to institutional religion."

Looking at the squirrels shaking the bare branches, I dredged up a long forgotten moment. "Do you remember back in the early Seventies, just after we were married, the man from behind the trees at U-Mass?"

She looked out the window, her eyes distant. After a long pause she nodded. "I do. He creeped me out. It was about this time of year, and we were walking across campus."

"What were we talking about," I asked. "Remember that, too?"

She laughed. "Amazing, but I do. It was alienation and reunion within the Marxist dialectic."

"Right. And the man?"

"He just appeared from behind a tree on the path in front of us."

"Remember what he looked like?"

"Only that even though it was fairly warm he was wearing a tattered overcoat, and one of those felt hats like Bogart wore in *Casablanca*."

"He only wore it in three scenes."

She sighed. "You would know that."

"What else do you remember about him?"

She rubbed her chin. "He had a crumpled peacock feather stuck in the hat band, and his sandals had socks under them. The cuffs of his pants were muddy, as if he had walked through the muck at the edges of Puffer Pond."

"Do you remember anything more about him?"

"He raised both of his hands and said hello."

"What else did he say?"

"He said, 'These are days of darkness,' and asked us if we knew Jesus."

"You grabbed my hand and pulled me away, saying you'd moved to Massachusetts from the North Carolina mountains to get away from people like him."

She tipped her head slightly to the right and smiled at me. "I did. They were all over the place in Banner Elk, self-styled preachers wanting to save souls while they were eyeing all the girls and young women. Hypocrites, with one hand out to take your money and another out to pinch your butt."

"You used to say they buried people in ten feet of biblical bullshit."

Laughing, she tapped the back of my hand. "They did. They were awful people."

"How many times have you said you could never live with somebody who believed in such crap?"

Moving her hand from mine and studying her fingernails, she did not answer.

I said, "Last night we were drinking martinis and arguing over Hillary versus Obama, and this morning you tell me this."

She laughed. "There's nothing in the Bible about not drinking martinis. I don't reckon they even had gin back in ancient Galilee."

"You're so full of shit," I said, grinning at her, relieved that she was joking. "You had me going for a moment."

Her smile disappeared as she looked me in the eyes. "It's not a joke, Tommy."

I sipped my decaf. It had cooled. Rising from my seat, I carried it to the microwave and put it in for ten seconds, giving me a moment to reel in my spiraling mind. The buzzer went off. I took my cup from the oven, steam rising from the surface, and carried it back to the table.

"Did this happen in the middle of the night," I asked her. "Did you wake up like Paul from his seizure on the Damascus road and think you had a revelation?"

She smiled. "I had a revelation, but it wasn't quite like that. It's been building in me for a while, but I couldn't talk about it. It was too private, too overwhelming. Like falling in love, you know. Things happen, you feel them, wonder about them and then *bam!*, all of a sudden you're in love."

"I remember what that was like."

Reaching across the table, she patted my hand again. "Me too."

"Taking Jesus into your heart was like taking me into it?"

"No. Jesus entered my heart. I knew he was knocking at the door, but I didn't invite him in. Doing that would mean I wanted a huge change in my life. I didn't, but he came in without being invited. With you, I asked you in. I chose you. Jesus chose me."

"I don't understand."

"You couldn't possibly, unless Jesus was knocking at the door of your heart."

"He's not."

Her face turned sad. "I know."

"What does this mean?"

"Everything to me."

"About us."

"Everything and nothing."

"Everything meaning..."

"I see the world in a new way. It shimmers with holiness, like diamonds of dew on the spring morning of life. The good news is you're an important part of that world."

"I shimmer with holiness like diamonds of dew on a spring morning?"

She laughed. "Sounds a tad overblown, doesn't it?"

I nodded, not knowing what to say. She watched me, her head tilted, as if waiting for a response. Her face looked as it always did to me over the thirty-six years we had been together: familiar, beautiful. When you love a woman as I love her, as long as I have loved her, she becomes the embodiment of the concept of beauty. I knew her, and could anticipate her moods and needs, as she did mine. Now it was all changed, utterly changed. I feared something terrible had been born.

I equivocated. "Not overblown. It just doesn't sound like you."

"Like the old me," you mean.

"Like the you I know."

"Like the one you knew. I'm different, renewed." She paused and looked into the air between us. "Recreated."

"You're trying not to say born again."

"It's not necessary to say it. I know what I feel, what I've become."

"When I asked you what all this means, you said everything and nothing. You talked about everything. What about nothing?"

"That's inexplicable. When Jesus entered my heart it didn't mean anything in the normal sense of meaning, and that's why I said it meant nothing. In itself, it just is. It is itself. When I said everything, I meant that everything had changed, that nothing could be the same."

"Where does that leave us, me?"

"That's the other part of nothing. Nothing has changed in the way I feel about you, or in the way I'll be with you. We're where we've always been, man and wife, parents, property owners, partners, lovers—the whole ball of wax."

I finished my coffee. It was cool again, as if the heat had been sucked out of it. Standing, I leaned over to kiss her cheek. Before I reached her, she turned her face upward and made three kissing sounds.

"About that man from behind the tree," she said. "When I think about it now, I believe he had walked on the surface of Puffer Pond that day. He was a sign of what I would come to, a prefiguring, if you would, of how Jesus would sneak up on me some day, jump out from hiding and enter my heart, batter my soul and make me new."

"You don't look battered."

"You have no idea of what I've gone through to come to a point where I could tell you any of this." There was a tinge of indignation in her voice.

"I had no idea that Jesus was hanging around at all."

"He is always hanging around."

After nearly a minute of silence, I said, "I need to get out of here, take a walk and think."

"I tell you the most important thing that's ever happened to me and all you want to do is to take a walk and think. Thinking won't help, Tommy. Thought has nothing to do with opening yourself up to holiness, to the divine. You have to abandon reason and jump into the unknown."

"I thought our life together was the most important thing that ever happened to either of us."

"It is, insofar as this world in concerned. I'm talking about eternity."

"I love you," I said, and touched her shoulder. She tried to smile, but said nothing.

At a loss, I walked outside and stood on the street, Tuckerman Court, named after a Nineteenth Century Greenfield poet, Frederick Goddard Tuckerman who had been a friend to Emerson and Thoreau, admired by Tennyson, and who today could be forgotten were it not for Poet's Seat Tower, which overlooks the town, and for the local poetry contest that commemorates him. The day was gray and a cool wind blew sand and dust that swirled in the street, rose in small eddies, and settled back onto the pavement, only to rise again with the next little whirlwind. The first nubs of crocuses showing through the ground were surrounded by clumps of snow I had shoveled from the walk after the last storm, an early April surprise. Behind the clouds, the sun was a worn white orb with no warmth, no color.

At least a dozen red-tailed hawks rode the thermals over the neighborhood, which sits on the edge of Highland Park, several hundred acres of woodland reaching down to the Connecticut River that separates Greenfield from the town of Montague, its banks a corridor bringing wild life from the forests and surrounding farm land into town. The hawks soared high above the still-bare trees. Individuals would swoop down, talons extended, to grasp a squirrel or chipmunk, another bird, anything in this season of scarcity to sustain them in their migration back north. I watched them for a long time, envious of their graceful movements in the way humans have always envied hawks and eagles, longing to ride the winds with their seemingly effortless beauty. My reflections were broken by the sound of sirens.

A moment later, three police cruisers and two fire trucks ran through a nearby intersection, nearly sideswiping a city bus at the corner. The sound faded and the bus moved on, revealing two men standing at the curb beside a telephone pole. The taller of the two pointed up the street, toward where I stood at the edge of my property. The second one nodded, and they stepped from the curb and started in my direction. I watched them move through swirling sand and dust, the smaller one walking with a limp. The other kicked at a plastic soda bottle lying at the side of the street. Zig-zagging his way, he followed the bottle as he kicked it along, the pursuit slowing his progress, turning it into what seemed to be random movement.

There was no one else visible in the neighborhood. Several blocks away, a dog barked, and was answered by others scattered around the area. A low flying plane buzzed above the trees, headed for a landing at the Turners Falls airport, a few miles across the Connecticut River from Greenfield. The two men continued up the street making no sound other than that of the hollow pop of the bottle each time it was kicked, and the noise it made scuttling over the pavement covered with sand from the winter road treatments.

I was suddenly seized by an inexplicable need to chase the men away, as if they represented a nameless threat to my security, my safety. Stepping into the street, I held up my arms, waving my hands at them.

"Get out of here," I yelled. "Go away."

They stopped. The bottled rolled back down the street and came to rest by the curb. The two men and I stood in the middle of the street in silence, separated by less than thirty feet. The dog barked again, but none of the others answered its yelping. The two men resumed their movement toward me.

"What's the matter with you," the shorter one said. As they drew closer, I could see their features. The shorter one was clean shaven with dark curly hair sticking out from under a knitted wool cap. His shoes were dusty and worn, and he wore a navy style pea-coat and khaki pants. The other was dressed in what appeared to be a camel hair overcoat and a tan fedora. The hat's brim was turned up, and the collar of his coat was flat against his shoulders. He looked out of phase, like someone who knew what to wear to achieve an effect, but didn't know how to wear it. With a thick mustache and heavy eyebrows, he looked as though he could be Saddam Hussein's cousin. He smiled at me from his position downhill.

I could not say what was wrong and continued to wave my hands, telling them to go away. They did not stop and quickly came even to where I stood.

"Geez, buddy," the smaller one said. "You gotta problem."

I nodded. "I do."

"Maybe we can do something about it," he said.

Just then the one in the overcoat stepped close to me and punched me in the stomach. Clutching myself, I bent over and tried to catch my breath. The smaller one kneed me in the jaw. I rose as quickly as I had bent over, but before I had a chance to react, the smaller one flashed a knife in the air beneath my nose.

"Why are you doing this," I asked.

"Why not," camel hair said, speaking in what could have been a Middle Eastern accent. "If we weren't doing this to you, we'd be doing something like it to someone else."

"It's a lucky day," pea-coat said.

"I don't feel lucky," I muttered.

"Perhaps, but we do," camel hair said. "Slice him, Randy."

The knife flew through the air, and I felt it slide into my shoulder. A moment later the pain registered, and I groaned.

"For a little bit there, I was afraid he wasn't going to make any noise," camel hair said.

"You got no faith in me, Joseph," Randy said. "I always make them hurt, and my hurts make them groan and cry before it's over." He kicked my feet out from under me and I fell to my back on the street. The white pitiless sun glared from behind the clouds.

"I should never doubt you," Joseph said.

"Never," Randy said. "Now what?"

"Kick his head in."

Randy's foot reared back and came toward my face. Blinding pain burst in my head. I curled up, raising my hands and arms to protect myself as Randy continued to kick me, landing painful blows in my rib and my chest. Then, as I was lying on the street, the pavement rough against my cheek, he drew his leg back and kicked me again in the head.

"You're going to be all right," a nurse said. "Two men beat you badly, but a neighbor saw it through her window, yelled at them, and called 911."

I ached all over, and the wound in my shoulder was like fire.

"Who," I asked, not knowing what I was asking: who beat me, who saved me, who the nurse was. It was just a word sent out into the air, a vocalization of my survival.

"We don't know who did it, Tommy." It was Jan. She sat by the side of my bed, a book open on her lap, wearing her white lab coat, a stethoscope hanging around her neck. "It was Mrs. Minsky who saw them and called the police. By the time they got there, the men who beat you were gone."

I tried sitting, but pain raged through me. Before I fell back I noticed the book in Jan's lap was a Bible, her hand resting on an open page.

"You've been here three days," Jan said. "They didn't know if you'd wake up, but I kept praying."

"I can't see well, and I hurt like hell."

I heard her take a long loud insuck of breath. "They punctured your left eye."

"It'll be all right, though," I asked.

"I'm sorry, Tommy." She spoke in her professional voice, flat, unemotional, speaking an indisputable medical truth. "It was done with a knife, and they stabbed your shoulder, but that wound is minor."

Reaching for my eye, I felt a large bandage over it. I tried to sit up but fell back, groaning in pain. "Jesus fucking Christ," I said, and began sobbing.

"Jesus had nothing to do with it." Her voice was tinged with reproach.

I shut my right eye. The image of the pale white sun was burned into my brain, and I lay there looking into its colorlessness as I willed the pain into recession. It was there, but distant, waiting for my vigilance to slip so it could resume dominance over me.

I must have slept. When I opened my eye, Jan was standing in the doorway talking with two men, one a uniformed police officer.

"Hi," I said, waving at her.

She came to my side and took my hand. "These men would like to ask you about what happened the other day."

I nodded my assent, and they came to stand beside my bed.

"Mr. Rutherford," the one in civilian clothes said, flashing a badge. "I'm Detective Lenny Bourbeau, and this is Officer Novak. I know you're hurting and confused, but I have to ask, do you remember what happened?"

"Like it's a movie running behind my eyes... my eye," I said, giving him the details, starting with the fire engines and cruisers, and ending with a description of Randy's foot coming toward my head. He wrote in a small spiral notebook as I spoke.

"Other than you, no one's seen these guys," Bourbeau said.

"What about Mrs. Minsky?" Jan had moved back into the room and stood next to the detective.

"She saw two figures beating Mr. Rutherford, but she couldn't give me any description of them. They're ghosts."

"First Jesus enters my wife's heart, and then I'm beaten up by ghosts."

"That's what I call perps with no description, guys that no one's seen." He ignored my comment about Jesus and Jan's heart.

"I saw them."

"Three days ago, and your description of them is the first one we've heard. My guess is that they're long gone. Someone probably hired them to do a number on you."

"Who'd do that?"

"You've asked my question to you."

"I don't have a clue."

"Tommy doesn't have an enemy on the face of this green earth," Jan said.

"That true, Mr. Rutherford," Bourbeau asked.

"There are people who don't give a rat's ass about me, one way or the other, mostly students who got lower grades than they believed they deserved. But someone who'd do this? I can't imagine who it could be."

He closed the notebook, slipping it into his jacket pocket. "We'll keep on the lookout for the assailants, Mr. Rutherford, but I don't expect we'll find them. I think they were hired to do a job, and left town as soon as that woman yelled at them."

"Mrs. Minsky," Jan said.

"Yeah," Bourbeau said. "Her."

"Now what," Jan asked.

"Your husband's got to try to think of someone who'd hire guys like that to work him over," Novak said.

"And that's it," I said. "You're throwing it back on me to solve this?"

Bourbeau's tone was sympathetic. "Times are tight, Mr. Rutherford. All the town's budgets are strained to the breaking point. The police force is down several members, just like other departments. Look at the schools, over a mil in the red, the fire fighters, the DPW. We do what we can, but there just isn't enough money to go around."

"Iraq," Jan said.

"Exactly," Bourbeau said. "It's a Bush war that's sucking the country dry. I'm sorry, but unless your husband can think of who wants him down, maybe out, and why, we can't do much. The ball's in your court."

He nodded to Novak, and after a few inconsequential pleasantries, they left.

I stayed in the hospital for two pain-filled weeks. Not only had I been stabbed in the shoulder and lost an eye, I had a ruptured spleen, a bruised kidney, and five fractured ribs. Our daughter Miriam called every day from her home in North Carolina, where she had gone weeks after graduating from Smith, saying she needed to explore her maternal roots and gather folk songs and stories. She earned an MA in history from Appalachian State University, and was now teaching at Watauga County High School in Boone.

Jan stopped by regularly as she made the rounds of her own patients and attended births at all hours. She took me home on a Wednesday, practically carrying me up the walk to the front porch, where I collapsed into a chair. I didn't have enough strength to go inside for twenty minutes. Green shoots had begun to appear on the bushes in the front yard, and the cardinals were singing as they flitted in and around them.

Jan sat on the arm of my chair and rested her hand on my good shoulder. "I've been giving your beating a lot of thought, Tommy."

"Me too, and I'm damned if I can come up with anybody who'd be behind this."

"Maybe there isn't anyone."

"Somebody did it."

"Those two men did it."

"Randy and Joseph."

"Exactly. Randy and Joseph did it, and that could be all there is to it."

"But why? There has to be a reason, somebody who wants me hurt or dead, like the detective said."

"Maybe it's nothing more than they saw you and decided to do what they did, a random act of evil."

"I can't accept that."

She sighed. "I didn't think you would."

We sat there, the only sounds those of the birds singing. A fat robin hopped across the lawn. Soon the air would be sweet with the odor of maple blossoms.

"With one eye, the world is flat," I said.

"With two eyes I found it flat." She didn't say that Jesus had changed all that for her, but I heard the implications in her phrasing and tone of voice.

"Even with me to love you?"

She kissed the top of my head. "Even with that. But without your love it wouldn't just have been flat. It would have been drained of color and without pleasure and humor."

"Glad I'm good for color and pleasure and humor."

"You always were."

When at last I found the strength to go inside, I stood in the hallway and looked at our house. It was home, a haven we had created. Every painting on the walls, every photograph of family members going back generations lining the stairway to the second floor, the furniture—some I'd had since childhood, some we'd bought at auctions, tag sales and antique shops, rugs we'd bought and rugs we'd inherited—all insulated us from the world, padded this nest we had made within the house we bought thirty years before.

I plopped on the couch and closed my eyes. The phone rang.

"It's Miriam," Jan said, passing me the receiver. "I'm going to fix us some lunch." She left the living room, and I put the phone to my ear.

"Hey, Mimi," I said.

"You all right, Daddy?"

"Fine, Mim. You?"

"I didn't get mugged," she laughed.

"It's good to be home. Hospitals are no place to have to spend time, unless you work there like your mother, of course."

"I'm coming up to Greenfield. I want to see for myself that you're all right."

"You don't have to do that."

"Yes I do."

"I'll be fine."

"But you're not fine yet," she said.

"I'm all right. Alive."

"I've got a flight from Charlotte to Bradley Field tomorrow, and I've reserved a rental car. I should be home by four or five."

"I look terrible, and I won't have a glass eye for months, not until the wound heals. It's pretty ugly."

"Don't you wear a patch?"

"I do."

"Bet you look like Captain Hook."

"I don't think he had an eye patch."

"I bet you look like some kind of pirate."

"Maybe."

There was a long silence, the dead air sound of an open phone line without words.

"Why did this happen, Daddy?"

"Wish I knew, sweetie."

"Mom said it was an act of random evil."

"I don't believe in evil. It's a theological construct."

"Is she all right?"

"Your mother?"

"She sounds really weird when I talk to her."

"This has been hard on her, trying to look after me, worrying, and doing her own work at the same time."

"It's not that. There's something she's not telling me."

"It's not about me. I'm fine. A little battered, but fine." I didn't say anything about her mother and Jesus. Jan would have to handle that.

We talked more. Miriam asked questions, and I assured her everything would be all right. After we hung up, Jan brought in egg salad sandwiches and juice. We ate, but said little. After she took the dishes away, I lay back on the couch, and was soon asleep. When I woke it was dark. There was a note from Jan on the coffee table, telling me there had been a difficult birth and she had been called to the hospital, and that a plate with dinner for me was in the refrigerator. All I had to do was nuke it and eat. At the end was a line of X's and O's, hugs and kisses, but the slashes of the exes were upright and horizontal, rather than the usual slanted lines.

Two

I stretched out on the couch and turned on the television. Smug commentators spoke without analysis about the economic meltdown, the race for the Presidency, and the latest sex scandals involving prominent politicians, avoiding substantive discussions of systemic problems by describing their accompanying symptoms, never linking the current economic meltdown to the disaster of the President's tax and war policies. My professional pride piqued, I flicked the set off. Easing myself from the couch, I hobbled to the kitchen to put my dinner in the microwave.

As I waited for it to heat, I studied a photo of Jan and me taken in Paris three years earlier. We stood by the Seine, facing the Musée d'Orsay. The museum is behind the photographer, a young English woman passing by who we'd asked to take the picture. The Seine is hidden by a wall.

Jan looked radiant; I looked weary. We had come from the d'Orsay and my mind was fuzzy from trying to take in too much art in too short a period of time. Not so with Jan. She could spend days in a museum, although her taste ran to Renaissance painting. I stood for twenty minutes taking in Van Gogh's self portrait, marveling over the thick brush strokes and the shadows they created on the adjacent brush strokes and on the surface of the canvas. She briefly looked at it, and then went on to another painting, and another, not lingering over anything, but restlessly moving through rooms where masterpieces failed to capture her for more than a moment. "Tomorrow we go to the Louvre," she had said, just before the English woman snapped the photo. Touching her face in the photograph, I pondered her preference for Botticelli over Van Gogh.

The phone rang.

"I'm going to be home late." Jan spoke in a near inaudible murmur. "Things aren't going well. We lost the baby, and the mother might not survive."

"Sorry," I said.

"Yeah. See you when I get home. Love you."

"Back at you," I said, but she had already hung up.

There was little I could offer in the way of solace. From experience, I knew Jan would be distraught for days over the baby's death, and should the mother die, she would be inconsolable, second guessing everyone in the birthing room, blaming herself for not making arrangements to be there as soon as the woman went into labor. Life would not be easy for days, but soon other patients and happier outcomes would boost her spirits, submerging any remaining anguish over events she could not control.

I took my plate to the living room, returned to the couch, and clicked the TV back on. Using the remote, I went to the menu for on-demand channels. Surfing through HBO's offerings, I considered the new George Carlin special, *Everything is Bullshit and it's Bad for You*, but skipped over it, my aching body and mind unprepared to deal with Carlin's psychic pain. I passed on *La Vie en Rose, Bernard and Doris*, and clicked on *Happy Feet*. Ten minutes later, bored by the mindless cute joy of the movie, I turned the TV off and pulled my pain up the stairs to the bedroom.

Stretched out on the bed, I picked up a book Jan had left lying there, Karen Armstrong's *History of God*. She had been reading it the night before, judging from the book light clipped to the back cover. After giving it a brief look, I put it down on her night table.

The phone rang again.

"Hello, Thomas," a voice said in accented English.

"Who's this?" I did not need to ask.

"An old friend. A blast from the recent past. You must remember me."

I didn't respond, but I didn't hang up.

"It's Joseph. You surely haven't forgotten me so quickly. I am speaking to Professor Thomas Rutherford, correct?"

"I remember you," I said, my voice a croak.

"I'm sure you do."

I hung up the phone. Less than a minute later, it rang again. I ignored it. After four rings, the answering machine in the downstairs hallway picked it up, and I listened as my voice drifted up the stairs and into the bedroom, asking the caller to leave a message, promising to return the call. Then Joseph's voice kicked in. It was loud, and I heard every word.

"You shouldn't hang up on me, Thomas. Pick up. I know you can hear me. Pick up the phone. I'm just calling to see how you are. I read in the newspaper all about what Randy and I did to you. My friend sent me the article. You do know my friend, right?"

I picked up the phone. "Who? Who's your friend?"

Joseph laughed. "I thought that would get you back on the line."

"Who put you up to this? Why did you hurt me?"

"Think of it as payback."

"Payback for what, to who? It doesn't make any sense. Who's behind this?"

"Who or what, Thomas? Does someone have to be behind everything?"

"You said a friend had sent you a newspaper article."

"Perhaps that was just to get your attention. Perhaps I have no friends. Oh, there's Randy, of course, but he's not really a friend, more of a collaborator, isn't he?"

"Why," I asked, the word covering more questions than I could ask.

"How would you describe your life, Thomas? Good? Bad? Just okay?"

I thought about his question, about Jan and Miriam, about our house, my job teaching Political Science at the University in Amherst, the pleasure I got from my students, the good caring work Jan does as a physician. We had a ski cabin in Vermont, enough time-share weeks in Virgin Gorda to allow us to spend each January in the Caribbean, and comfortable, reliable cars. We prepaid our winter heating bill and often took summer vacations trips to Europe, to Provence or Umbria, often to the west country of England. We would rent villas with friends and explore cities and countryside.

"I have a wonderful life."

"Bingo. Bob's your uncle. Shazam. You do have a wonderful life, don't you Thomas, my boy? Any idea about Randy's life? About mine?"

I was silent, sure he would continue without prompting.

He did. "Let me tell you: Randy's life is a mess. He was shot up badly in the first Gulf War. He's got one lung, one testicle, a prosthetic left foot, and no toes on what remains of his right foot, all thanks to a land mine.

His state of mind's even worse. At night he can't sleep unless there's a light on in the room, the radio blaring, and the TV on mute, and even then he sometimes sees monsters slipping out from under the bed or beneath his closet door. His father was killed in Vietnam, his mother committed suicide when he was eight, his sister tried to have him committed, claiming that he was dangerous to himself and others. Of course he is. You're evidence of that, aren't you? And, to top it all off, his ex-wife slit his throat when he was drunk and stoned, damned near killed him. And that's small time shit compared to my life."

"What does this have to do with me?"

"I was born in Iran and my parents were both dead by the time I was nine, killed by the Shah's henchmen. After the Revolution, the conservative Muslims were doing all kinds of bad shit, and when I was ten, I was sent to America to live with my mother's sister and her husband in the Upper Peninsula of Michigan. The fucking son-of-a-dog beat me and buggered me until I bled. The only person who tried to protect me was my aunt, and he killed her and buried her body in the field behind the house, and nobody ever knew a thing about it. I ran away when I was twelve and lived on the streets in Detroit. You think your New England winters suck? Try sleeping in doorways a block from Lake Michigan and being the boy prey of every sicko pervert in the city."

"Who do you work for," I asked.

"I've been cut, shot, beaten into a coma, raped, jailed, I'm HIV positive, and I've had tuberculosis. With all that shit, I've still had to earn a living, haven't I? I've been a taxi driver, a dock hand, a gravedigger, worked in the sewers, dealt drugs, stuck up convenience stores, took a degree in philosophy, all at night. I've done all kinds of shit. Randy says I even killed a man, although I don't remember doing it. I don't remember a lot of things. It's a terrible thing, not being able to remember what you've done, isn't it?"

"I could never kill someone, but if I did I'd remember it. It would drive me crazy remembering, ruin my dreams, ruin my waking life, ruin me. How could I forget?"

"I'd have to forget. Who would want to remember something like that? What would be the purpose in remembering? Sometimes I almost remember terrible things, as if fragments of events flit around the edges of my mind, but before I can put them together they fade. Isn't that just terrible? Well, maybe not so terrible, if I think about it.

Why would I want to remember killing somebody? Forgetting our crimes and sins is the kindest thing we can do for ourselves."

Ignoring his question, I asked again, "Who do you work for?"

"You could call my employer a god of vengeance," he said. "And he's not satisfied that you've learned your lesson."

"What lesson's that?"

"You'd know if you'd learned it. It's a lesson about the meaning of life, but don't worry, teacher won't forget you." He hung up.

I lowered the receiver to my lap, holding it in a tight grip as the dial tone buzzed. I rested upright against a pillow, staring at a family portrait of Jan, Miriam, and me propped on the dresser. It had been taken by my brother, Barry, two years earlier on our thirty-fifth wedding anniversary. We were all smiling, ready to break out in laughter at Barry's corny jokes.

"How would you describe your life," Joseph had asked. I said I'd had a wonderful life, but wonderful wasn't the right word. Life as I live it isn't wonderful, or terrible, or anything so broad, so sweeping. It's complicated, but I've never wished to be anyone else, nor have I ever wished for my life to be other than it is. Would I have done some things differently had I known the consequences of my actions? Of course I would. I sure as hell wouldn't have walked out the door onto the street the day Jan told me Jesus had entered her heart.

As I tried to think of other things I might do differently, given the chance, the phone beeped three times, and a woman's voice came from the receiver. "Please hang up and try your call again. If you need assistance dial your operator. Please hang up now. This is a recording." The message repeated three times, and was followed by a string of loud pulsing beeps. I put the phone back in the cradle and unplugged it from the wall.

I did not sleep. For hours, I sat in my study trying to think of anyone who might wish me harm: students I'd failed for plagiarism, lack of preparation, or sheer stupidity; college administrators frustrated by my insistence that they adhere to the letter of our collective bargaining contract; townspeople angered by my very rude opposition to the expansion of the local shopping mall. By two in the morning, I had a list that filled a page. I looked it over. There wasn't a person on it who I believed hated me enough to turn me over to the likes of Joseph and Randy. There were many who would laugh uproariously should I slip in the mud and land on my face, or be delighted to know I had gotten drunk, crashed my Lexus into a telephone pole, and ended up in the hospital to spend weeks recovering from my injuries before reporting to District Court for trial and sentencing on a DUI charge. Like anybody, I had earned the dislike of many, but not, I felt sure, their hatred.

So who had set Joseph and Randy on me?

Jan was home by 6:30. I heard the garage door motor whine, and the creaking of the door as it rose, followed by the sound of her car door slamming shut. I was halfway down the stairs when she came through the front door, her hair limp, her face gray, almost ashen. She shut the door behind her and dropped her purse and keys on the hall table.

"I lost them both," she said, her voice small and quaking. "The mother died twenty minutes ago. I thought she was going to be fine, and she just plumb died."

"I'm sorry," I said.

"She's in a better place, you know."

I didn't know. "Are you all right?"

"For now. She's with her baby."

"That would be a comfort," I said. I had never heard her speak in such a way. It gave me a glimmer of understanding as to how opening her heart to Jesus might be a practical bulwark against these moments, rare but unavoidable in her work. Watching patients die is far more taxing than seeing a favorite student totally blow a final exam.

"Do you mean that?"

"As an observation, not an acceptance."

"The husband's furious."

"Of course he is."

"I'm going to get sued."

"You have malpractice insurance."

"That's not the point. You didn't see his face or hear the rage in his voice."

"He needs to blame someone right now. He'll get over it."

"I don't think so."

"Was something wrong?"

"Supposedly one of the nurses had alcohol on her breath. I didn't know about it until I was getting ready to leave the hospital."

"Maybe she was blown away by what happened, and took a drink afterwards to calm her nerves."

"It was the father who told me about her. He said he noticed it when they were both leaning over his wife, trying to resuscitate her. She coded when he was in the room with her, and he wouldn't leave when they came with the crash cart. He insisted on helping, no matter how urgently the crew tried to get him to leave."

I helped her out of her coat and led her to the couch.

I sat beside her and put my arm around her shoulder. She stiffened, then relaxed.

"I don't want sex."

"I'm not offering you sex, just an arm around your shoulder."

"With you that sometimes leads to sex."

"Sometimes it's just intended to let you know I love you."

"And sometimes you want me to show you how I love you by spreading my legs."

"You didn't used to mind sex."

"I was younger. It's harder now."

"For both of us, but I do feel abandoned in that realm of our lives. It's been months since we've made love."

"I should have seen it coming, Tommy," she said, redirecting our conversation, turning it back to the death of her patients. "I should have been watching her closer."

"Why weren't you?"

"There were two other women in labor, and a newborn in respiratory distress."

"You were busy."

She pulled away from me and stood. "It comes to the same thing. A mother and her baby are dead."

"I'm sorry," I said again. It sounded small compared to what she was feeling, but there was nothing I could do, nothing I could offer beyond telling her I was sorry.

"How's the baby with the respiratory problem?"

"Fine."

"That's something to be grateful for."

"I need sleep," she said, and started up the stairs.

Following her to the bottom of the staircase, I rested an elbow on the newel post and watched her ascend with slow steps, moving like someone pulling herself through water. She disappeared around the landing, and I went to the kitchen to make a pot of coffee. I started to spoon decaffeinated grounds into the pot, then changed my mind, and went for the real stuff. It would be a long night. The coffee maker hissed and popped, dribbling the brew into its pot. When it was done, I poured a cup, and walked up the steps to work in my study.

I heard Jan's voice. Our bedroom door was open, and I looked in and saw her sitting on the edge of the bed, the covers thrown back. Bent nearly double, head resting in her hands, she rocked back and forth, her hair rumpled and the sleeves of her flannel nightgown twisted around her arms.

"Please, please, please Jesus, please," she repeated several times as I stood unseen in the doorway. "Please Jesus, bring light, bring light and understanding, Jesus, please help me understand and cope with this."

Embarrassed by watching her in a moment of such vulnerable intimacy, I slipped back downstairs and returned to the kitchen, where I sat until the coffee pot was empty. My mind and body jagged from the caffeine, I struggled to understand where the currents of life had brought me. Was I in danger of crashing into uncharted and deadly shoals, in danger of being lost in a vast unknown open sea? Or was I setting out on new and unexplored waters; my landfall, should there be one, distant, frightful, and mysterious?

I thought of Jan and Jesus, of Randy and Joseph, of the changes they had wrought upon my previous and reasonably well-ordered life. More than half a decade earlier, a terrible and terrifying event had taken place; falling towers and ruined planes spewed human and structural debris into the air, littering the streets below, clogging the lungs of thousands who stood by.

The catastrophe surged into the world's consciousness, altering the manner in which those it touched conceived of the meaning and possibilities of their lives, mutating all our futures. The attack that September was concrete in its immediacy and horror, abstract in its long range affects, as the future is always abstract, a concept unborn, one of anticipation not satisfaction. As it recedes into the past, the attack becomes an ever-fading national memory, resting in millions of minds, superseded by millions of more pressing and personal matters, yet influencing our thoughts and actions in ways we often fail to recognize.

Jan, Jesus, Randy, and Joseph were immediate and concrete, a present that belied all I had anticipated from life, pressing and personal matters that would not recede and must be faced and understood if I were to once again take control of my future.

Three

Miriam bounced into the house late the next afternoon, her blonde hair pulled back into a loose ponytail. Leaving her bags by the stairs, she plopped herself on the couch next to me and planted a wet kiss on my cheek.

"Where's Mom," she said.

"At the hospital. Babies come at inopportune times."

"Who's the detective watching the house for you?" She took my hand and patted it, much like I had done hers so many times when she was a child sobbing over some kind of injury.

"What detective? I haven't asked the police for any kind of protection."

"I was sure he was a detective. He was very nice when I passed him on the sidewalk, and he said he was here to serve us to and not to hesitate to call him if we needed anything."

"What does he look like?"

"Tall, he had a mustache and an expensive looking overcoat, and wore one of those old timey hats, like Clark Kent wore, you know."

"A fedora."

I rushed to the window and looked at the empty sidewalk. "I don't see him," I said, my voice faint.

"He was just there." Miriam stood beside me and pointed toward the sidewalk. "He was standing by that telephone pole."

"Did he have an accent?"

She tilted her head. "More like a trace of one rather than a real accent."

"Did he say anything else?"

She shook her head. "But he knew who I was. He spoke to me before I turned down the walkway to the house and called me by name. I figured you had told him I was coming."

"He's one of the men that beat me, Joseph."

She paled. "He acted so pleasant."

"He's dangerous. Don't believe in appearances."

"What'll we do?"

"First, I call the police." I pointed at her bags. "Get yourself settled upstairs while I talk to them. You mother cleaned your old room for you."

She grabbed her bags and ran up the stairs while I made the call and got the dispatcher. I asked for Detective Bourbeau.

"I need protection," I said when he came on the line. I described Miriam's encounter with Joseph, and the call he had made to me the day before.

"You're sure it was the same man," he asked.

"I didn't see him, but my daughter described him well enough, and it was certainly the same man on the telephone."

"What do you want us to do?"

"Post someone to watch the house."

"I'm sorry, but there's no way to do that. The department's budget is strained beyond capacity already."

"So what do I do?"

"If you see him again, call and we'll try to pick him up. But we don't have the resources, financial or manpower, to post someone out there to watch your house."

"That's it? That's all you can do? Where does that leave me?"

"Being very careful." I heard him take a breath. He spoke again before I could respond. "You could hire someone, an off-duty officer, a private security firm."

"That's not much in return for my property taxes."

"Tell me about it. My kids' music teacher just got laid offm and the art program hardly exists anymore. I'm sorry, Mr. Rutherford, but have you noticed how dirty the streets are? Public Works has less than a third of the employees they had five years ago."

The phone rang almost as soon as I hung up.

A man's voice asked, "This Doctor Travis's house?"

"It is," I said.

"Not for long," he said. "Tell the bitch that everything she has is going to be mine. I'm going to sue her ass off. She won't even be able to sit down."

"Who's this," I asked, but the caller had already rung off.

I am not a violent man. Prior to being hammered on by Joseph and Randy, the last fight I was in happened over fifty years ago, at recess in the fifth grade. Sammy Devlin pushed me to the ground.

"You don't get up and fight," he had said, "I'm gonna kick the living shit out of you."

I got up swinging. He knocked me down.

"Get up," he'd said again. By then we were surrounded by kids, summoned by Sammy's friends who yelled, "Fight, fight!" Every time I got up, Sammy knocked me down. I was saved when a teacher intervened and took me, dirty and sobbing, to the nurse's office.

Sammy was twenty-two when he aspirated on his own vomit and died in a jail cell. I admit to having felt some joy when I learned of his death. I still take a small amount of pleasure when I think of it, even though I don't believe in engaging in violence, nor do I believe I have been guilty of violent acts.

That said, I wanted to kill Joseph and Randy, and I knew I would kill anyone who came after Jan or Miriam.

"So, Daddy," Miriam said when she came back downstairs. "What's going on with Mom?"

"You need to hear it from her."

She pulled a straight-backed chair across the room and, placing it directly in front of me, sat and looked me in the eye. "She's not having an affair, leaving you, or anything like that is she?"

"She's on a path very different from my own."

"What does that mean?" Her voice was sharp, suspicious.

"Talk to her. She can explain it. I can't."

"You're scaring me, Daddy."

"Whatever's going on with your mother isn't what we need to be frightened of."

She pressed me, I parried her questions. When she saw I wasn't going to budge, she became quiet. I took the opportunity to change the subject.

"How's your search for Appalachian roots coming?"

"Did you know my great great grandmother was a Cherokee?"

"I didn't."

"At least that's what my cousin Lenny Hicks believes."

"People believe in all kinds of things," I said.

"I asked if he had any birth certificates, dates, things like that, but he said there weren't any, so I don't reckon I'll be able to prove anything. I'll just have to take it on faith that he's right."

"You don't reckon?"

She laughed. "Roots. I've picked up a lot of phrases. Lenny and the other cousins are also great musicians and storytellers."

"You like it down there?"

She nodded. "In spite of that fact that there are too many churches and preachers. On an eight-mile stretch of Gap Creek, a back road near Johnson City, I counted eight churches and a barn, with 'Yes Jesus Yes' written on it in bright yellow letters six feet high."

"That's a lot of churches," I said.

"And some of them have more than one preacher. Just out of curiosity, I went to a couple of churches like that, and all they did was prattle on about sinful movies and sinful music and sinful alcohol and sinful politicians and sinful this, sinful that. Jesus, it was awful."

"Roots," I said. "That's where your mother came from."

"I can understand why she left."

"And yet you went back, and you're still there."

"I love the people, not the preachers. The mountains are beautiful and there's wonderful music and stories there. I want to learn them all. Maybe I'll write a book." Her eyes shone with an enthusiasm reminiscent of Jan's during her early years in medical school, when she was first learning the mysteries of the human body, filled with wonder at its complexity and resilience, and excited by her growing knowledge about it and the thought that she would be in a position to work with it, help in curing its ills and discover more of its secrets.

"Roots," I repeated. "I can't imagine living anywhere but here."

"Tell me what's up with Mom," she said.

"I can't. You'll have to ask her."

"Rats," she said.

We both laughed.

Jan was home by seven. Miriam rushed into her arms, and they headed off to the kitchen for cocoa and conversation, just as they used to do when Miriam was a girl. Stretched out on the couch, I basked in the familiar comfort of their voices, alternating between conversation and laughter. In spite of the pains from my injuries, for a brief while I convinced myself all was well, that Jesus and Randy and Joseph and the bereft husband and father threatening a malpractice suit against Jan were figments and would fade as life's normal routines reasserted themselves.

Jan sent out for Chinese. When a driver from the local taxi company delivered it, I leapt from the couch at the sound of his voice, sure it was Joseph. He was gone by the time I got to the door.

"It wasn't," Miriam said when I asked. "Don't you think I would have done something, said something if I recognized him?"

After dinner, Jan stretched and yawned, shrugging at Miriam. "I'm ready for bed. Sorry, Mimi, but I'm plumb exhausted."

"There was a phone call earlier," I said. "I think it was from the husband whose wife and baby died. He said, and I quote, that he was going to sue your ass off."

"I'm not worried. Nothing can touch me now," she said, and started upstairs.

Miriam watched her, eyes wide.

"What's that about," she said, when Jan disappeared around the landing.

"What did you and your mother talk about?"

"About school, my teaching, the cousins, and about Gramps. He's not doing well since Gram died."

"Nothing else?"

She shook her head.

"Nothing about herself?"

"She mentioned something about going through some changes, but when I asked what kind of changes, she said we'd talk about it later, when she wasn't so tired. Is something wrong, Daddy? What kind of changes is she talking about? Is she sick?"

"I don't think so. Keep an eye on her over the next couple of days while you're here."

She nodded slowly. "Why won't you tell me anything else?"

"Talk to your mother."

At the University the next morning, I found Joseph sitting outside my office. Still wearing the camel hair coat, the fedora perched on his knee, he jumped to his feet and put a restraining hand on my arm as I turned to leave. He had shaved his mustache.

"It's all right, Thomas. I mean you no harm."

I pointed to my eye. "That's harm, fucker, and you meant it. You fully intended to do everything you and Randy did to me."

"That's all in the past. This is a new day, and we need to talk."

"Fuck you and fuck the past." I took out my cell phone and opened it to call security. Grabbing it, he flipped it closed and handed it back to me.

"Hear me out. Then, if you still want to call someone, do it. I won't stop you."

Students and other faculty members passed by. The adjacent office doors were open, my fellow political scientists at their desks, some reading, some talking with students. There were enough people around to restrain him should I need help.

I pointed to two chairs in the hall next to my office door. "We can talk here."

"I want to be your friend," he said, resting on the arm of a chair.

I laughed. "That's not possible."

"Anything's possible, Thomas. Let me be your friend."

"For the sake of argument, should I agree—which there's no chance in hell of happening—why would you want to be my friend? What kind of friendship are you offering? Are you trying to soften me up so I won't press charges against you and Randy for beating and blinding me?"

"I will never harm you again, whether or not you take me into your heart as a friend, and I'm certainly not trying to soften you up."

"With friends like you—" I started to say.

"Who needs enemies," he finished. "Such a trite expression, and what do you know about friendship?"

"I have friends."

"I didn't mean to imply you were friendless. It was a philosophical question." He eased himself from the chair arm into the seat. "Aristotle spoke of three kinds of friendship: those of pleasure, those of utility, and those of virtue."

"Where does friendship between us come in, and what does any of it have to do with you two assholes pounding the shit out of me and leaving me blind in one eye?"

He waved a hand in the air. "I'll come to that. First, concede that being a friend means having a distinct concern for the object of the friendship."

"Object or subject?" In spite of myself, I was intrigued by his conversation.

"Subject would be kinder. Will you concede my first postulate?"

"For the moment." He had caught me. That I agreed friendship implied concern for the friend meant our relationship had morphed—for the moment—from assailant and victim to partners in a complex dialogue.

He smiled. "Good. Now, I consider that this unique concern for a friend is a kind of love."

"You're offering me love?"

This time he laughed. "The Greeks spoke of agape, eros, and philia. I'm not speaking of eros, but philia, agape even, although there is a distinct philosophical difference between them, I'm never sure of which is which. In this sense I'm not speaking of agape as Christian theologians have distorted it, but more in the sense of love for humanity, which to some is not terribly different from philia, which can be seen as affection and esteem towards friends, family, neighbors, and one's country or the world."

"How does beating me fit into this?"

"It doesn't, exactly."

"Exactly?"

"Perhaps it leads to this."

"To friendship?"

He shrugged. "It's difficult to predict what will happen in this world."

I thought of Jan letting Jesus enter her heart. "I'll accept that postulate."

He looked satisfied. "Now, back to Aristotle's friendships of pleasure, utility, and virtue. Do I love my friend for the pleasure she affords me, the tasks she performs for me, or the sterling virtue of her character?"

"The first two are selfish. You're taking something, pleasure or service. The third seems more abstract, more honest."

"More altruistic?"

"I don't believe in altruism."

"Why do you think Randy and I attacked you?"

"Someone paid you to do it."

"No."

"You enjoyed it."

"At the time, yes. In retrospect, no."

"So, you feel guilty about it?"

"Not at all. It happened and it's over. That's the end of it."

"Not for me." Again I pointed to my eye. "Why did you do it?"

"You asked me that before, on the phone, and I didn't answer you. Now I do. I did it because I failed to recognize the virtue in you. I did it because you represented something unattainable to me."

"Why me?"

"You were there, standing on that tree-lined street with its big houses, their yards and gardens, and all the other things that such streets and homes imply to people like Randy and me. It was clear you had just emerged from your own lovely home on that street."

"It wasn't a planned attack? I wasn't your target?"

"It wasn't planned, but you became our target simply by being there and letting us see you."

"Letting you see me? It wasn't a decision, a choice to let you see me."

"But we did see you."

"So it was a random attack."

"Random or inevitable, depending on how you choose to construct the world. It doesn't matter. I'm offering you my friendship based on the virtue I now see in you. I will love you as a friend and make you the recipient of my own virtue."

"And your friend, Randy?"

"Randy was never a friend. He was a companion."

"But you care about him. I could tell that by your description of his life when you called me."

"He was an abstraction, his life representative of many."

"How does he fit into this offer of friendship?"

"Randy doesn't matter. He is in the past."

"If I refuse to be your friend?"

"It won't matter. I am now your friend. I will love you and I will protect you and your family with the same ferocity with which Randy and I attacked you." He extended his hand for me to shake.

"I'm not your friend," I said, refusing his hand and reaching for my cell phone.

"And I am yours. I've done some checking around on you already. I understand that an angry patient has been threatening your wife."

"He's not a patient. His wife and baby were her patients. They died."

"She must be upset, your wife."

"I won't discuss with you anything about my wife, my daughter, or any of our personal matters."

"That's an admirable, if somewhat short-sighted, position. I intend to be helpful." He rose and left the area before I could dial security. By the time an officer came, Joseph was gone, and no one was able to find him on campus.

"What kind of shit is this," I said.

Detective Bourbeau sighed into the phone. "There are all kinds of crazies around here. Go down by the railroad tracks behind the Main Street Cumberland Farms store. The woods are full of them, living in tents, in refrigerator boxes, in shanties made out of all kinds of cast-off stuff, from car doors and hoods, to sticks and canvas. Used to be we could commit them to state hospitals and see that they were taken care of, sheltered from the weather and fed, but no more. We gotta let them wander the streets of town, panhandling and living like animals in the woods."

"I don't think Joseph lives in the woods. He's well dressed and groomed."

"Who knows? There was a lady a couple of years ago lived in those woods with her boyfriend in the rusted-out hulk of an old Buick they managed to haul in there, god knows how. Both of them are crazier than shithouse rats. They got what little money they could scrounge by up deposit bottles and cans. She saved up enough to buy a Y membership, and would shower there every day, washing her clothes as she did. There wasn't a person on the street looked at her but didn't just assume she was a middle class housewife out shopping. One morning, folks at the Y found her dead in the parking lot, and called us. She'd had a heart attack the night before and froze to death where she collapsed. It wasn't until we tried to identify the body and notify next of kin that we found out where and how she lived."

"You think Joseph is one of those crazies, living out in the woods?"

"No reason to believe he is, or isn't. I just mean you can't tell jack shit from the way somebody dresses. Sometimes I think you can't know jack shit about anything."

The rest of the day went like any other at the University, predictable and comfortable. I taught classes, met with students in my office, attended a committee meeting where people talked more about process than substance, and fended off questions about my eye and the beating. On the drive back to Greenfield I rode in silence along the River Road, catching glimpses of the Connecticut River through the undergrowth, passing farms and the newer homes that have been springing up in Deerfield in recent years.

Normally on the ride home I listen to NPR, matching their analysis of political events with my own and that of my colleagues, and I tried paying attention to *All Things Considered* during my first few miles out of Amherst, but I could not concentrate on what was being said. My conversation with Joseph that morning played over in my mind. I was increasingly unsettled by his statements, *I am now your friend. I will love you and I will protect you and your family with the same ferocity with which Randy and I attacked you, and I intend to be helpful.* I could not avoid comparing them with Jan's assertion that she had accepted Christ, that Jesus entered her heart and told her to follow him the rest of her days. Jesus and Joseph promised unwanted and inconsistent change to a life with which I was quite contented.

Crossing the bridge into Greenfield, I saw the spring rain and the snow melt had swollen the Deerfield and Green rivers, flooding the golf course situated on the low ground between them. A few minutes later, as I passed the crumbling rental houses on Deerfield Street, I remembered something else Joseph had said outside my office, *I'm offering you my friendship based on the virtue I now see in you.* What kind of virtue had he seen? I have never thought of myself as virtuous, nor had anyone told me I was. It was not a word I used, other than in the sense that something may come to be by virtue of its something. Virtual is a term more common, virtual reality, she is a virtual gem, but virtue?

The word is related to virile, with its connotations of strength and manliness, its meanings broad, including conforming to a standard of right, connoting morality and moral excellence. It is linked to the order of angels, in the sense of a celestial hierarchy, and to the beneficial quality or power of a thing. With its sense of manly strength, valor, and courage it is associated with commendable qualities and traits, and thus to merit. Two further senses of the word are the power to act, or potency, and chastity, especially in a woman. Manliness, potency, and female chastity, mingled in a single word and used to describe some unknown quality Joseph claimed to see in me and use as the basis for his undesired and perhaps dangerous friendship. And which sense of virtue embodied that mysterious aspect of my being that so appealed to him?

Flowers for Jan came at dinner time, with a note, "Everything will be fine." It was signed "A friend."

"Yellow roses, how nice," she said, reading the card.

"Who're they from," I asked.

She turned the card over several times. "There's no signature. It's a mystery, I guess."

Miriam looked up from her meal. "There are too many mysteries around here, Mom. What in the hell is going on with you?"

Jan's face reddened.

"You've been acting flat-out weird, and Dad won't tell me why. He says I have to wait and hear it from you." Folding her arms over her chest, she tapped her foot. "Well, Mom, I'm waiting."

Jan placed the vase of roses on a side table in the dining room and, sitting back down at the table, met my eyes and smiled. "I'm not sure your father approves."

"I don't," I said.

She sighed, reached across the table, and patted the back of Miriam's hand. "It's complicated and simple."

Miriam looked confused. "Both at the same time?"

"I've found Jesus," Jan said.

Miriam laughed. "Under the bed, or in the refrigerator with the leftovers?"

"It's not funny." Jan's words were clipped and angry.

"Nothing funny about it," I said. My words were sad and resigned.

Jan glared at me.

"You've found Jesus," Miriam said.

Jan nodded. "And it's complicated because none of you can understand it, simple because it just is. He entered my heart and changed my life."

"That's simple?"

"The simplest thing in the world. All I had to do was accept him. He did all the rest." She took a sip from her wine glass. "And now I'm safe by virtue of my faith in his love and understanding and eternal protection."

Miriam took a deep breath, releasing it in soft shudders. "I don't get it, Mom. You've never had a good word to say about religion."

"I agree that much of the world's evil is done under the guise of religion." Jan tightened her lips. "My relationship with Jesus is beyond religion; it's a matter of the heart."

"And..." Miriam said.

"It's like that old hymn, 'What a friend we have in Jesus, all our sins and griefs to bear!' He's bearing mine. Without him I couldn't go on. Losing Tildy Mathews and her baby was a final blow." She rubbed her eyes, but I saw no tears. "I've seen too much sorrow, too much death: women with cancer of the uterus, still-born babies, sterility driving women and men to desperate and incredibly expensive measures so that they might have children. Sorrow and loss. I couldn't take it any more, and now I don't have to. He lifts my sorrows and cancels my losses."

"Mom," Miriam said, drawing the single word into a statement of exasperation and confusion.

"I know it must be a lot to take in, given my history."

"It's a shit load to take in."

Jan sighed. "I understand."

"You've always been the sanest, most rational person I know. I've depended on you for advice and direction. Saying that Jesus cures your sorrow isn't exactly sane."

"Reason, as it's defined in our world, isn't exactly sane."

"You're talking in riddles, Mom."

I looked from one to the other as they spoke. Miriam's objections echoed mine, but I knew their discussion would end like all those between believers and their challengers end. It came more quickly than I expected.

"You couldn't possibly understand unless you've had an epiphany as I have," Jan said.

"Aha." The sound was out before I could check it. They both looked at me as if I had uttered a profound obscenity.

"That wasn't helpful, Dad."

"Your father's a doubting Thomas." Jan smiled at her use of my name.

"It's impossible to have a meaningful discussion with anyone who believes they've had a true supernatural experience," I said. "Their system shuts down, admitting only the facts that fit, and reconfiguring those that don't in order to make them fit."

"That's an insult to my intelligence," Jan said.

"Mom's right. It doesn't advance the discussion." Miriam's voice was stern, and in it I heard my own severe tones, so often directed at her childhood antics.

I felt sick. The ground my marriage had been built upon was crumbling, along with the solid life I thought I was living.

"I can't take this," I muttered, and stood up, resting my hands on the table just inches from Jan's elbow.

She hummed a few bars of "What a Friend We Have in Jesus," then sang:
Do thy friends despise, forsake you? Take it to the Lord in prayer;

In His loving arms He'll shield you; you will find a solace there.

"That's not particularly helpful either," Miriam said.

"Sorry. You're right. I was being snotty." Jan reached for my hand, taking it softly in hers and stroking my wrist with her forefinger. "I love you, you know."

I nodded, my throat so tight I feared my voice would squeak if I said anything.

"This will all sort itself out. My faith will become another aspect of our life. It could strengthen it, if you'd let that happen. You wouldn't even have to accept Christ."

"I won't," I said.

She gave me a sad smile. "Maybe."

"Don't let this come between you." Miriam's voice was pleading.

"It won't," Jan said.

"It has," I said at the same time.

I tried reading myself to sleep that night. The strain was great on my remaining eye, and I soon had a walloping headache. Downstairs, I swallowed three aspirins with a beer, and turned on the television. The news channels were filled with stories of the Pope's visit and the primary elections. I couldn't find a movie that appealed to me and settled on a re-run of *Murder, She Wrote*, tuning in too late for the set up, and falling asleep before the resolution. When I woke at 5:30, it seemed like an expression of my life.

Four

Coffee and email at quarter of six in the morning were terrible. The coffee, left over from the day before and heated in the microwave, smelled like old athletic socks and tasted worse than it smelled. There were two unread emails in my box. The first left me saddened. It was from Jack Richardson—a colleague from earlier days when we were both starting our careers in a small college in New Hampshire—telling me about the death of Nick Miller, who had been the school's head librarian.

Tom, it started. I thought you should know that Nick Miller committed suicide. Here is what I know about it. Royall Davenport (English faculty) had been visiting Nick periodically since Marie's death and their daughter Lizzie's stroke. Nick retired five years ago, was in poor health, seemed depressed and, according to Royall, had become quite reclusive over the past year and a half. Royall had gone to visit him yesterday and met him driving away from his house toward the lake. He followed him, and when they parked by the state beach he found that Nick had a shotgun in the car. Royall said he was a little concerned, but that it wasn't unusual for Nick to have a gun with him. He had a large collection, you know, maybe a hundred or more, hand guns, antique rifles, and even some modern heavy duty weaponry: M-16s, Kalashnikovs, things like that. After a short conversation, they agreed that Royall would go to Nick's house and wait for him to come back home. (Royall is also a photographer, and wanted to take some photos around Nick's property.) When Nick did not follow him home, Royall became concerned, and went back to the lake to see about him. He found the body there. Nick had left a note with directions on how to find his son, Jason, and a sealed letter for Jason. A memorial service is scheduled for Saturday evening, April 26, at the Episcopal Church in New London.

Death sucks. We need to make the most of our time, and I hope to see you soon. It has been too long. Love, Jack.

I had seen Nick over the years when I would go back to New Hampshire to visit Jack and walk around the old campus where he still taught. I keep in touch with people from my past. It's important. My first wife, Andrea, and I moved frequently in our younger years. Seeking the perfect teaching job, I was uncomfortable in small private colleges which were often run by presidents who had been in place for many years and considered the schools their private fiefdoms. During the eight years of our marriage, I never stayed in one place for more than two or three years. I made good friends at the many places I lived and taught. Visiting with them over time, seeing their children grow, their careers mature and end as they retired, has been a way of integrating my life, keeping it a continuum rather than a series of episodes with no pattern, no direction other than that of my seemingly eternal dissatisfaction.

Nick and I weren't close, but I appreciated his caustic sense of humor, his intellect, and I admired the way he had built up a fine library collection, despite the financial limitations of a small college with a minimal endowment. He had also designed and overseen the construction of a new library building. His story is an example of the random nature of life and the way its horrors can devastate one family. Marie had taught biology at the college, but was laid off because of a bookkeeping error that led the trustees to believe the school was in greater financial distress than was true. Nick had been convinced the resultant stress of losing half the family's meager income was a factor in her developing the non-Hodgkin's leukemia that killed her less than two years later. As she lay dying in the Dartmouth-Hitchcock medical center, their twenty-three-year-old daughter Elizabeth, who had just given birth to her first son, had a stroke from which she never fully recovered. Jason's fiancé was killed a year later in a skiing accident at Mount Sunapee.

Nick carried on for seven years after Marie's death and Lizzie's stroke before driving down to the lake with his shotgun and a load of despair that I can not begin to imagine. In comparison, my own problems seemed small, but I could not escape the thought that they were just as random and potentially as disruptive of my life in their own way as Nick's had been of his. Jan's sudden declaration of her faith in Jesus, my battering and partial blinding at the hands of Joseph and Randy, and Joseph's discovery of a virtue in me that led him to proclaim his friendship and intent to help me, all seemed to spring from the chaos against which we attempt to structure our lives.

The second email frightened me.

Dearest Friend, Joseph wrote. *It was a pleasure to visit with thee at the University earlier yesterday. I hope thee had a restful night and trust this electronic epistle finds thee well. I also trust thee will understand and respect my choice of the second person singular objective in addressing thee in our written communications. English is my second language and I have thus found it necessary to be far more attuned to the value of its subtleties than many native speakers. I am exceptionally appreciative of this particular usage as it has been historically employed by various English speaking spiritual and religious groups, as well as the intimacy similar forms imply in other languages. In utilizing this intimate form I hope to underscore the level of affection and esteem I have for thee.*

Should thee doubt this, I am confident my future actions will permanently lay thy doubts to rest and assure thee of the good will I hold toward thee and thy family. I was quite impressed, by the way, with the poise and beauty of thy daughter, Miriam. It was a pleasure to meet her the other night, and I hope I might soon again have such a splendid opportunity to bask in the glow of her company. Who knows where that could lead? Perhaps someday you may be my father-in-law.

Your friend, indeed, Joseph.

Relieved that Miriam was returning to North Carolina, I deleted Joseph's email and forwarded Jack's to Jan, sure she would want to know about Nick. I hoped the meaningless tragedies of the Millers' lives might force her to reconsider the implications of the irrationality of her Jesus trip.

The next few days were calm. Jan mentioned Nick's death only briefly, as if to let me know she had registered it, but she gave no appearance of grief or sadness over the news. After Miriam left for the airport to return to North Carolina, tooting three times as she drove her rental car away, I returned to what had been my normal routine before Jan's announcement and Joseph's appearance. I taught my classes and worked in the library, researching a study I was doing on politics and reason.

I am a bit of a pariah among the traditionalists in the Political Science department, for several reasons. I have been vocal about the erosion of academic standards in the University in general, as well as in the department, a problem related to our students' increasing lack of preparation and academic ambition. In addition I reject the concept of scientific analysis of political behavior, convinced most people's political behavior is, at its core, erratic and illogical. Polls give snapshots of where voters might believe pollsters want them to be at any given time, or where they have drifted in the currents of the moment, reacting to transitory passions and events rather than analyzing issues and their implications.

With regard to polls, I am convinced people also tailor their responses to leading questions, with momentary obsessions influencing their interpretations of those questions. The pollsters and the polled are in a political dance, the music for which has little to do with real issues and everything to do with how both partners wish to be perceived, and like most music, its effects are emotional and untidy, not intellectual and coherent.

The current political season has been particularly upsetting to me. I have said that in the midst of other cycles, but at sixty-two, I am tired of thinking about campaigns, elections, governments, wars, and the whole goddamn ball of wax, which has become more chaotic as the result of cable news channels distracting the public by playing up insignificant events and claiming they are of momentous political import.

Three days after Miriam left, I woke up at 3:30 in the morning. Jan was standing in front of our bedroom window, silver white in the light of the full moon, her outstretched arms reaching toward the sky. Her hair streamed down her back, and I was caught up by her deep and amazing beauty, as I always am while looking at her in moments when she is unaware of my gaze. Selfishly, at those times, I want to touch her, make love with her, and speak to her of her loveliness. Even more selfishly, I refrain, not wanting to destroy what seems like an instant of perfection.

Breathing softly, regularly, like a sleeper, so as not to alert her that I was awake and staring, I watched her, consciously trying to fix the image in my mind so that I'll be able to call it up some day when I am old and, perhaps, alone in a small room in a nursing home, my days winding their way down toward death and, I fear, annihilation. Since the loss of my eye, I see in but two dimensions, but when I see with my memory or my imagination, images are three dimensional.

I watched Jan for a long time. She stood unmoving until a cloud obscured the moon, returning her hair and shoulders, her face, to the gray of night. I closed my lid and envisioned her in a fullness my one eye could not grant. I held the image like a jewel as I listened to her step back from the window, climb into bed, and pull the covers over her shoulders. I still watched her, washed with silver moonlight standing before the window, as she lay beside me and began to snore.

I was headed out of town toward the University the next morning when my cell phone rang. It was Bourbeau.

"I need you to meet me at the hospital," he said.

"I'm on my way to work."

"It's important. I need you to look at a body in the morgue. It may be the other man who assaulted you."

"Randy?"

"He fits the description. It won't take long."

I agreed, made a U-turn in the driveway of a junkyard, and headed back into town. He and Novak met me at the entrance of the Franklin Medical Center.

"There's been an odd wrinkle with Joseph," I said as we walked through the hospital, and told him about his non-negotiable declaration of friendship.

"Makes sense in a weird way," Bourbeau said.

"How so?"

"Wait until you see what we've got downstairs."

We walked the rest of the way to the morgue in silence. They led me to a body lying on a gurney, the body bag unzipped to the neck line.

"So," Novak said.

"It's him, Randy. How did he die?"

"It looks like the killer shot him in the knee to disable him, and then stabbed him in the heart," Bourbeau said. "We got an anonymous call from a fisherman who found the body snagged by rocks and brush in the Green River, down by the Ten Mile Bridge. We don't know if he was killed there or floated down."

"Any idea who did this," I asked.

"Who do you think?" Bourbeau zipped the body bag, closing it over Randy's face.

"I can make a good guess, but why?"

"Like I said, it makes sense now. He did it to prove his friendship to you, let you know he's made sure that Randy'll never hurt you again." He made a wide Gallic shrug, his arms stretched out. "Who knows how this creep's mind works?"

"But you can't prove he did it."

Novak shook his head. "We don't even have the bullet. It passed through him and is probably buried in the ground wherever they offed him, or at the bottom of the river. We'll never find it."

He patted the body bag where the dead man's shoulder was. "The upside is that now you got only one asshole to worry about."

"That is a plus," I said.

"Call us if he shows up again," Bourbeau said.

"You mean it's all up to me?"

Bourbeau scratched his head. "You got to be proactive on this, given the finances in the police department. Remember, we can't spend our time looking for him."

Annoyed at what struck me as his cavalier attitude toward the problems resulting from the police department's fiscal straits, I turned and left them standing by the body. Headed back to work, I was passing the University's sod experiment lab on the River Road in Deerfield when my cell phone rang again.

"I see they found my gift to you," Joseph said.

"Killing a man is a gift?"

"Don't make assumptions. He could have killed himself. You might consider the fact that I found the body and placed it where it would be found as the gift."

"You mean he shot himself through the heart."

"Could be."

"Did he?"

"I'm not sure." He sighed into the phone. "There are things too painful to remember. I would think that killing a man is one of them, so if he didn't shoot himself through the heart, if I did kill him, I have no memory of it. Therefore, I can say with a clear conscience that I didn't kill him, and allow myself to believe I am telling the truth."

"Even if you did kill him?"

"The truth is what I believe."

I felt like my head was going to explode. "You are fucking crazy."

There was a long silence on the other end. I pulled onto Route 116 and crossed the blue bridge over the Connecticut River into Sunderland.

"That was uncalled for, cruel," he said, when I reached the stop light on the other side. His voice was sharp, accusing. "Friends don't talk like that."

"I am not your friend." I screamed the words into the phone and slammed it shut.

It rang repeatedly as I drove the rest of the way to Amherst. At the end of the day, I decided to leave it in the office and let the battery run down. I did not want to be in touch, to have people able to contact me any time, no matter where I was. There are too many links to the world's demands without cellular phones adding to the stress. This one I would break.

Jan did not accompany me to Nick's funeral, which was short and sparsely attended. The minister, a thin man with sunken cheeks, almost cadaverously pale, spoke in generalities about Nick, ending his remarks with a plea for donations to the college library.

"I understand Nicholas was a librarian and his son, Jason, has asked that in remembrance of this, you make a donation to the college library. Books, after all, are our cultural memory." He held up a Bible, waving it over the few people in the pews. "The greatest memory of all," he said and began to pray.

Even fewer people went to the burial in the pine sheltered corner of a small rural cemetery along the sloping shore of Lake Sunapee in Newbury. Jack Richardson was there, along with a handful of men and women I didn't know. Nick's daughter Lizzie stood propped up by two of the men. Her right side was paralyzed, and a thin stream of saliva drooled from her mouth. She did not look at the coffin, her eyes fixed on the tree line beyond the cemetery. Jason made a few terse remarks, and after the coffin was lowered, he tossed a shovelful of dirt and stones into the grave. Several other people took handfuls of dirt and dropped them in.

"His few remaining friends are pissed that he shot himself," Jack said later. We were sitting at a bar in New London, and I had commented on how few people turned up for the funeral. "Plus, he left the college five years ago, and he'd been so reclusive since Marie died, I think most people had forgotten about him."

After two beers, I stood up and clapped him on the shoulder. "I've got a two-hour drive back to Greenfield."

We shook hands, and I left him sitting there, holding his hand up to signal the bartender to bring him another beer. When I reached the parking lot, Joseph was leaning against the driver's side door of my car.

"You're a hard man to get in touch with these days," he said, waving his cell phone at me.

"I left my phone at the office. I'm tired of being in touch, and I'm really tired of being in touch with you."

"I know." He reached into his pocket and pulled out my cell phone, tossing it to me. "I found it on your desk and charged it up for you."

"How did you know I was here, and how did you get into my office?"

He shrugged. "I know how to find out things, and I know how to do things. I especially know how to find out things about my friends and do things for them."

"I believe I've made myself clear about our friendship," I said, reaching for the car door handle.

He stepped aside and smiled. "You'll come around. No one can resist me for long."

"Or they'll end up like Randy?"

He made a tsking sound with his tongue. "Poor Randy, but he was never a friend. We were companions for a while, but companions come and go. Friendship is forever."

"You killed him." I got into the car, shut the door and started the engine.

He shook his head, and spoke loud enough for me to hear over the sound of the motor and the closed window. "Not that I know of. You're not unhappy about his death."

Without replying, I put the car in reverse and pulled out of the parking lot. In the rearview mirror, I saw him standing beside the spot where my car had been. He smiled and waved the fingers of his left hand at me. As I turned the corner, he blew me a kiss. I drove home on back roads, and tossed my cell phone into the sand at a road side quarry in Lempster.

During the 1950s, more a hundred thousand people in the United States built bomb shelters underneath their basements and back yards. By 1960, the government estimated there were over a million shelters, sturdy underground warrens of reinforced concrete rooms buried well below ground level that their builders believed would protect them from atomic blasts and fallout. Bob Rutske, who was running for sheriff in Michigan during the building frenzy, remarked that "To build a home today without a shelter, would be like leaving out a bathroom twenty years ago."

In the late sixties and early seventies, Jan and I, along with seven other students at the University, rented a farm house with such a shelter in Leverett, a rural hill town within easy commuting distance of Amherst. We converted one of the shelter's rooms into a root cellar and another into a marijuana drying chamber, saving the third for hiding draft resisters and soldiers who came to us after going AWOL.

If I had one now, I'd stock it with food and water, take Jan in with me, and lock the world out until our supplies were gone. With luck, when we emerged, Jesus, Joseph, and Tildy Mathews' bereft husband would have disappeared from the landscape of our lives. Driving south on Route 10, passing Keene and the hardscrabble farms and homes of southern New Hampshire, bumping over the decrepit main street of Winchester, I constructed an elaborate fantasy of the life we could live in our shelter: no news of the outside world, no visitors, only the two of us, taking turns fixing meals, reading, writing, making love, and finding each other once again.

That was the shelter I craved, normalcy, my life back in its comfortable groove, although I knew it would never be.

When I walked into the house following Nick's burial, it seemed as though Jan wanted the same normalcy. She was already home, the air full of the smells of cooking. She met me as I walked across the living room toward the kitchen and hugged me.

"I love you."

"I love you," I said, holding her close. She smelled of garlic and onions. Her hair tickled my nose, and I sneezed.

"Allergic to me," she laughed.

"Don't think so."

"You're not sure? I'm a doctor, you know. I reckon I could cure your allergies."

"How would you do that?"

"I have ways." She spoke with a deliberate mysterious tone, and smiled.

"Ways?"

"Ways. Don't ask, just accept." She whispered the words in my ear, her breath warm and exciting.

I pulled back, holding her shoulders at arms length. I realized we were speaking in code. If I broke it, the moment would pass, and we would be more alienated.

"If it gets any worse, I'll take your cure."

She pushed her way back in close and smiled. "You'll take it anyway. There's wine on the table and rack of lamb in the oven, garlic/horseradish mashed potatoes, and broccoli Dijon on the stove."

This wasn't normalcy. Jan was striving for something else. She hadn't been home cooking like this in more years than I could remember. Normally we would work together, throwing some kind of quick dinner together, or go out to a restaurant. She was courting me, and I was willing to be courted without asking why.

Later, lying beside her, Handel's *Water Music* on the bedside CD player, I stroked her arm. Her entire body rose and fell with a deep sigh.

"What," I asked.

She didn't reply.

I rested my head on her shoulder. "What?"

"Everything's fine, Tommy. Let's not talk."

"Everything isn't fine if you don't want to talk."

"I'm just happy in the moment."

"But not beyond the moment?"

She ran the fingers of her free hand through my hair. "Who knows what lies beyond any given moment?"

I thought of Joseph. "Not me."

"Let's do it again." She touched my ear with her tongue.

"Do what," I laughed.

"It. You know, it."

"I'm willing to try."

"Try? Thomas Rutherford, since when do you have to try?"

"Since I got old."

She pushed me away, got on her knees, and, straddling me, gave me a deep long kiss. "You better not act old tonight."

Afterwards we fell asleep. I awoke hours later, at three AM according to the red digital display on the CD player. Jan was sitting up, staring into the night.

"I love you," I said.

"I love you, too, but this doesn't change anything, Tommy."

I looked at her in silence, searching for her meaning. "Jesus is still in your heart, you mean?"

Her profile was sharp and clear against light from a street lamp. She nodded.

"He is."

"I suppose I'll have to learn to live with that."

"It's a blessing, you know." Her voice was testy.

I didn't reply.

She lay back down and faced me. I heard the rumble of a motorcycle pass by on the next street. I touched her cheek, and she placed her hand over mine, holding it there.

"I didn't want this," she said. "I would have given anything for it not to happen. It doesn't make my life easier. Harder, actually."

"But you wouldn't change anything now that it has happened."

She whispered, "No."

"If it helps, it makes my life harder, too."

"It gives me a kind of peace I've never known."

"It doesn't give me anything. It takes, if you want to know the truth."

"I understand."

"Do you?"

"I do."

She rolled over and turned on her light. "What do you feel?"

"Resentment. Loss. Sorrow."

"I wish you could feel what I feel."

"Christians have to say things like that."

"I'm not a Christian, Tommy. I don't go to church and I don't like preachers."

"What are you then, with Jesus in your heart?"

"Different."

"That doesn't tell me anything."

"It tells me everything, and it lets me bring my love to you, fully."

"It's sick." The words seemed spoken before I thought them.

"No." Her voice, barely audible, was angry. "It's not sick, but this obviously isn't the right time for us to talk about it." She turned off the light and lay on her side, facing away from me.

"I'm going to sleep. I've got early morning appointment, and I have to meet with the hospital review board at 11:30."

"The dead mother and baby?"

"Her name was Tildy Mathews. Her husband named the baby Angel, and had her baptized. I will be sued."

"What about the nurse with alcohol on her breath?"

"No one can prove anything. It's his word against hers. He reported it, but he was the only one to notice it."

She said nothing else, and in a few minutes, her breathing changed. Soon she was snoring lightly.

Five

"We've got to stop meeting like this." Joseph spoke as he approached my car in the University parking lot. It was the end of the day and I was preparing to drive home. A soft wind blew from the west, rippling the new leaves freshly out on the trees.

"It's not my choice." I clicked the remote key to unlock the doors.

"Pity." He opened the door on the passenger's side and slid into the seat before I could stop him. "We're going on a field trip."

I yanked my door open and leaned in, shaking an open hand at him. "Bullshit. Get out. I'm not going anywhere with you."

He leaned back in his seat and smiled. "You're not my only friend, you know. I have friends all over the world: in France, England, Russia, Azerbaijan, even back in Iran, to say nothing of the New England states, California, Texas," he paused and looked up, engaging my eyes, his voice even, without inflection. "I have a very good friend in North Carolina."

I wanted to hit him, but controlled the urge, not sure what would happen if I did. "What do you want?"

"Just to take you on a field trip."

"Leave my daughter alone."

"Of course. But then, I never planned otherwise. The daughter of my friend is my friend, and I'd be obligated to protect her from anyone who wished her harm, including me. I would have to commit suicide if I hurt her, or even tried to hurt her. I am a man of honor, Thomas, and you would do well to remember that. Now, get in the car and drive."

Worried about Miriam, I followed his orders. We drove west on Route 9 and turned south on I-91 at Northampton. At first we rode in silence. After a few miles, he turned on the radio and found a country music station.

"I hate what's happened to country music," he said. "It used to be truly country based, clever and basic, with fiddles, pedal steel guitars, banjos, and even autoharps. Now it's soft rock, with string sections, horns, drums, and trite lyrics. Just imagine what country music would be like today if Chet Atkins, rather than Hank Williams, had died in the rear of that Caddy back in '52."

"How do you know so much about our country music?"

He hesitated and cleared his throat. "It's listened to all over the world."

"Even in Iran?"

He rolled down his window and took a deep breath. "God, I love the smell of manure on fields, the maple blossoms, all that spring stuff." His accent was gone. He looked over at me. "I lied about all that Iran shit. I'm as American as you."

He even looked different, any trace of ethnicity suddenly gone from his face and carriage. It was eerie. "Why did you lie?"

"The right question is why am I telling you the truth?"

"And why is that?"

"Friends don't lie to friends, at least for very long. As my friend, you're entitled to the truth about me."

"You killed Randy."

He shook his head. "I don't believe I did."

"You're still saying you can't remember whether or not you've killed people."

"That's the truth. Why would I lie about it?"

"Why do you do anything?"

He sucked his teeth and looked out the window. "I don't know."

"You don't know?"

"No. I do things and sometimes I remember doing them, but I rarely remember why I did them."

"Like beating me in the street in front of my home and leaving me half blind."

"Like that, but not that." He paused, cleared his throat, and rolled up his window. "I know I did it. Well, Randy and I did it, and I regret it. I remember doing it and I rue having done it. I'm truly sorry, Thomas, truly truly sorry. I choose to believe it would not have happened if Randy hadn't been with me."

"You're saying it was his fault."

"I'm saying it wouldn't have happened if I'd been alone."

"It's the same thing."

"No, it's not."

"You are one crazy fucker."

He nodded eagerly. "I am. I am a crazy fucker. A dangerous, crazy fucker, if we're to judge from what Randy and I did to you."

"How can I not judge?"

He laughed. "I suppose you have to, although I'd rather you suspended judgment until after our field trip."

We were coming up on the Mount Tom overlook area. Reaching the exit, I pulled in and stopped the car. "Get out."

He looked at me, a faint smile playing around his lips. "This area is a notorious pick-up spot for anonymous male sex, you know."

"I know."

"And you want to deposit a straight male friend here?"

"How do I know you're straight, and why should I care one way or the other?"

He rested a hand on my knee. "We could make love here."

"I don't want to make love with you. I want you to get out of my car and leave me alone."

He pulled his hand away quickly. "You certainly don't think I'd want to have sex with you?"

"Don't know. Don't care."

"Drive," he said.

"Get the fuck out of my car."

He laughed again. "Get the fuck out of my car, but don't fuck in my car?" I glared at him.

"Drive," he said again.

"No."

He hummed a tune as he took a cell phone from his pocket. "What's the area code for Boone, North Carolina? 828?"

"You son-of-a-bitch," I said, putting the car in gear and pulling back onto the highway.

"I suppose my mother could be blamed for how I turned out. I wouldn't really know. I never met her, or my father. I was raised in a series of foster homes in Springfield."

"You want me to believe that?"

"It would be nice if you did. Coincidentally, that's the purpose of our field trip. Now drive and be quiet, so I can concentrate on where we're going."

We rode without speaking. Just past the bridge over the Connecticut, 91 curves sharply to the right and cuts through Springfield. He told me to get off at the Birnie Avenue exit, and directed me under the Interstate overpass and onto Springfield Street. We drove past Baystate Medical Center, and from there onto a series of back streets and finally onto Nevada Street, which dead ended after one block.

"Park here," he said, pointing to a vinyl clad triple-decker. "The good foster parents who lived here had a room in the basement they called the detention center. There were shackles fixed to the walls. There were between six and ten kids living here at any given time. My sister Nancy and I were here for five years, from the time I was four until I was nine. Every Saturday night, Papa Daigle, as he insisted we call him, would line us up in that basement and switch our legs with a car antenna. 'That's for anything you little shits might have done wrong this week,' he'd say, pointing to the shackles. 'It'd be worse if I'd've known what you did.' Once he found out I'd been stealing comic books from a store, and he put me in the shackles for two days. My feet didn't even reach the cellar floor. Sometimes my shoulders still hurt."

"I'm supposed to believe this?"

"Turn around at the end of the street. I want to show you another place."

After winding through more back streets, we finally came to a stop in front of a weed-covered vacant lot.

"The foster parents in the place that used to stand there took turns raping Nancy and me and two other foster kids. They threatened to kill us if we ever ratted them out, their words. When she was fourteen, Nancy hanged herself. The next night, the place burned down, and both the scumfucks died in the fire. The other kids all made it out safely."

"You burned the place and killed them."

He shook his head. "That's not how I remember it. The arson investigators said that Reverend Damon set the fire by smoking in bed. I do remember being happy about it. All of us were."

We sat there without talking. I stared at the lot. It was covered by scrub bushes with shredded plastic shopping bags on their limbs, scraggy patches of grass, broken bottles, and a rusty swing set, chains with no seats still hanging from the cross bar. Joseph got out of the car, came around to my side, and opened my door, motioning for me to get out. We walked to the middle of the lot.

He wrapped his hand around a chain from the broken swing and put it in motion. "This set was right here, this very spot, all those years ago. We weren't allowed to use it. The Damons had a niece and nephew who would come over sometimes for Sunday dinner with their parents. We'd be locked in our rooms those days, but my window looked out over the yard, and I would see those two kids swinging and laughing our here. I hated them."

He looked around, sweeping the air with an open hand. "I hate this town. It bills itself as the City of Lights. It should be called the City of Darkness, or the City of Knives and Guns, or the City of Fucked Over Kids."

"I'm sure there are more good people in the city than bad."

"It doesn't matter for shit. What Nancy, I, and hundreds of other kids suffered here is what matters. You and your neighbors in your big houses in little towns on your tree-lined streets don't have a clue about the lives of people in cities like this."

Back in the car, we drove for another ten minutes, and then stopped in front of a small house with a sagging front porch, its lawn and front gardens filled with weeds.

"This is the last foster home I was in. It looked a lot better then. I ran away, and I've taken care of myself ever since."

"What happened here?"

"We had good food every day, help with our homework, and it seemed that we were loved."

"Why did you run away?"

"I was afraid it was a scam to suck us in, make us trust them so they could turn around and hurt us."

"Did they?"

"I never gave them the chance. As I said, I ran away." He drummed his fingers on the dashboard and sighed. "Let's go. My car's back at the University. You can drop me off and go home."

"I find all this hard to believe," I said as I drove north on 91.

"As do I," he said.

"Because it's another lie?"

"Because it's true. I've never told anyone about it, never shown anyone those places."

"Why me?"

"The virtue in you. You're my friend because of that virtue. As my friend, I want you to understand me."

I spoke softly. I am not sure by using that tone if I was trying to spare his feelings, to approach him with some sympathy for what he said had happened to him, or if it was in an attempt at mollifying him. "I am not your friend. I could never be your friend. Even understanding your life, if that was your life, I can not be your friend. You beat me, blinded me, and would have killed me if Mrs. Minsky hadn't seen you and called the police."

"Good old Mrs. Minsky," Joseph said. "I send her flowers once a week."

"Why?"

"To thank her for saving your life."

"Saving it from you."

"From Randy and me. We were greater—worse, if you will—than the sum of our parts. I'm a better person without him. I'm a much better person as a result of my friendship with you."

I didn't deny his friendship. I didn't say anything. Nothing I could say would affect his obvious misperception of me and our relationship, which for me was that of victim and abuser.

"Now you know a version of my life." His speech was accented again, but this time it sounded more Slavic than Middle Eastern.

"Two," I said.

He gave me a sharp look. "Really? Two? I have been busy haven't I?"

Folding his arms over his chest, his head drooped, and we rode back to Amherst without talking, nothing but overproduced country music filling the car with sound.

I left him at the University and started home. Hungry, I stopped at the all-night diner on Routes 5 and 10, just off the 91 exit in Deerfield. A small group of truckers stood smoking outside the brightly lit chrome building, their rigs idling in the background, rumbling and sending diesel fumes into the air. I walked past them, taking a deep breath of cigarette smoke.

"Them truckers didn't bother you none, did they," the waitress behind the counter said as I came in. Slender, with muscular arms, her hair was dyed blonde, and she wore a low-cut blouse, her breasts tan and large and heavily freckled. There were four other people in the diner: an elderly man wearing dungarees and a tank top, his gray hair pulled back in a pony tail, and three boys sitting in a booth, college students judging from the calculus books they were hunched over.

"Why would they bother me?"

She wiped the counter with a well-used rag, and set a steaming mug of coffee in front of me. "You look like you could use that."

I took a sip, blowing on the surface to cool it as I drank. "Thanks. You don't know how much I needed it."

"Those guys outside don't mean to be annoying, but ever since the town banned smoking in restaurants, they stand around out there and smoke up a storm before coming in. Some people get bent out of shape over having to walk by them. You know how some of those Valley types can be."

"I enjoyed it," I said.

She laughed. "Oh, you did? Ex-smoker, I take it."

"It's been twenty-three years since my last cigarette. It was New Year's Eve, and I was on the beach on Anegada, a little island in the Caribbean where my wife and I were vacationing."

"Remember what kind it was? My last ciggie, ten years ago, was a Kent."

"I don't forget things," I said. "Remembering helps keep me sane."

"Remembering can make some folks crazy," she laughed. "So what were you smoking?"

"An unfiltered Pall Mall. I smoked it down until it burned my fingers. I sucked every last bit of nicotine from it that I could."

"Fingers all yellow, were they? Mine were."

"As yellow as the filling in that lemon meringue pie there." I pointed to a pie rack on a shelf behind the counter. "When I was finished, I tossed it into the ocean, and I haven't smoked tobacco since, so walking through clouds from other smokers can be a pleasure. It makes me glad I quit while at the same time gives me a little nicotine rush."

She gave me a knowing smile. "Never smoked tobacco again, eh? What have you smoked?"

I had to laugh. "Nothing. I've always been afraid that if I smoked anything else, I'd start in on cigarettes again."

"What a shame. Since Connecticut River tobacco's not a big cash crop around here anymore, there's some awful good other kinds of smoke growing in the Valley."

"I need to keep my head on straight. Especially now."

"Problems?"

"More than I want to think about."

"A little weed now and then might help."

"I don't know what would help right now," I mumbled.

Her eyes widened at my morose tone. "You want to talk?"

I shook my head. "Think I'll just have a piece of the lemon meringue pie."

She cut me a large slab and refilled my mug. Leaning both elbows on the counter, she took a deep breath. "My name's Kathy Shepherd."

"Tom Rutherford," I said.

She shook my hand. "You look familiar."

"I've been in before; I live in Greenfield."

"Sooner or later, you see most people that live in the area, either in here or shopping in Greenfield or 'Hamp. Been married long," she asked, pointing at my ring.

I sipped coffee and nodded. "A long time."

"Lucky. My husband, Warren, died two years ago, cancer, after twenty-seven years together. He was a strong man, big, farmed over in Whatley, mostly tobacco, but we raised a little asparagus, some tomatoes, brocs, caulies, corn, shitloads of zukes and summer squash, along with other veggies, some of it off-beat stuff: bok choy and the like. Had a little farm stand along the highway right by the hot dog stand off exit 22. One day, Warren came in from the fields and said he had to pee out there and there was blood in it. We went up to the hospital in Greenfield and the docs got all upset, put him in for tests. The next day, they did an exploratory operation, sewed him back up, and came out shaking their heads, saying he had cancer in his bladder, cancer in his prostrate, cancer in his gut. Hell, Tom, there was cancer all over the poor son-of-a-bitch."

Not knowing what to say, I shook my head and made a sympathetic grunting sound.

"Damn straight," she said. "One day he's out working in the fields, the corn knee high and the tomatoes getting red. He pees a little blood, and two months later he's in the ground and I'm stuck figuring out how to keep the farm." She gestured around the diner. "So here I am, working this damn counter at night and farming during the day."

"I'm sorry. It must be hard."

She shrugged. "It's a pain in the ass, but it's all right. I mean, hell, you never know what's going to happen. You're out there living your life, and the fucker comes along and yanks it all out from under you, and there you are trying to figure out what to do next."

"What fucker's that?"

"God, that's who. The fucker of all fuckers. Makes me feel a little like Job, you know?"

"I don't know much about the Bible," I said.

"Wouldn't do you much good if you did. More coffee?"

I had finished the pie and drained my mug. "Any more and you'd have to wipe me off the ceiling."

Just then, the truckers who had been smoking outside came in, laughing and talking loud. They all greeted Kathy by name, and clambered into two booths near the college kids. The diner was immediately filled from the odor of stale smoke clinging to their clothes and bodies. The boys sniffed the air, closed their books, and headed for the door.

"Hey, you owe me for the coffee," Kathy yelled after them.

"It's on the table," one said over his shoulder, pointing back at the booth.

"Yeah, right," she said. "And probably a quarter tip. Twits drive me nuts," but she was smiling, and said it with a trace of affection.

"How about some coffee, Kath," one of the truckers called.

"Yeah, yeah, Moe, be right there." She turned back to me. "The fucker'll cut you off at the knees before you know what happened, and Heaven'll echo with his horse laughs."

Jan was still gone when I got home at 11:30. The answering machine was blinking. The caller ID read Charles Mathews. I pushed the play button.

I sure as hell hope you got a good lawyer, bitch, because you're going to pay for my wife and baby, and you won't have a damned thing left when I'm done with you.

After erasing the message, figuring Jan didn't need to hear it, I poured half a glass of vodka, added ice, and topped it off with a little orange juice. I flicked on the TV, lay down on the couch, and watched a re-run of *M*A*S*H*, followed by two episodes of *The Andy Griffith Show*. I fell asleep in the middle of a *Sanford and Son*, waking when Jan came in.

"Where have you been," I asked.

She rubbed her eyes. "I had two deliveries tonight, and a third woman in labor. I fell asleep at the hospital, and just woke up a few minutes ago."

"What about the third woman?"

"She'll probably deliver in the morning. They'll call me if it looks like it'll come sooner." She sat next to me on the couch.

"What happened with the review board?"

"Nothing. They agreed that Tildy's death was unavoidable."

"That's a relief."

"It doesn't make me feel any better. She's still dead, and so is the baby, and I'm going to be sued."

"That's *pro forma*," I said. "The insurance company'll take care of it all."

"I'll have to testify."

"They'll settle out of court."

She sighed. "Probably, but it doesn't matter. There'll be depositions, and it'll be ugly with her husband. He's been leaving nasty messages at my office." She looked over at the phone. "I'm surprised there aren't any here."

"There was one. I erased it. He's an asshole."

"He's a broken-hearted twenty-two-year-old kid who's lost the love of his life and his baby. He's entitled to act like an asshole. I just wish he wouldn't direct his anger at me." She fell backwards, resting her head on the couch. "I thought Jesus would make this kind of thing easier for me."

"He hasn't?"

She shook her head. "Not in the way I'd hoped. I suppose he wants us to work things through on our own. It looks like the best I can hope for is knowing he's with me, pulling for me, giving me strength."

"So am I."

She reached up and touched my cheek. "I know, and I'm grateful."

We sat there for a while, not talking, scarcely paying attention to *The Jeffersons* and *Good Times*, and climbed upstairs at 3:30. I was so tired I felt sick, and fell onto the top of the bed fully clothed.

Six

My ruined eye ached. It was a clear, bright, spring Saturday morning, the sun warm, the air holding traces of the northern chill lurking around the corners of New England's weather, even on the finest of summer days. Jan and I had been hiking the High Ledges in the Patten section of Shelburne, part of the Audubon sanctuary where grew a wide range of wild native plants, including many varieties of orchids and ferns. An extensive trail system runs through the hardwood and pine forest at the Ledges, many of its byways leading to panoramic views of the Deerfield watershed, stretching from Shelburne west into the Berkshires. Standing at the overlook on the edge of the escarpment, with my good eye I looked at the valley below, Mt. Greylock distant in the background. Three hawks soared in the updraft, feathered kites rising and falling effortlessly in the flatness of the two dimensional vista spread before me.

Other hikers stood nearby, some passing us as they walked the trails, all speaking in the hushed voices people use when they feel the beauty of their surroundings can best be appreciated in quiet. Some held cameras, still and video, moving their lenses over the landscape as they tried to capture the splendor of the moment. From the woods beyond the preserve came the sound of someone playing modal tunes on a flute. I put my hand on Jan's waist and pulled her close. Her hair moved slightly in the wind, and the scent of her perfume was as sweet as the spring wildflowers. Still, my ruined eye ached.

"This is as nice as it gets," she said. "No beeper, no voices over the PA calling me, no patients. Just the sun and breeze, the woods and trails and this view."

"No Joseph and no Charlie Mathews."

She rested a hand on mine and gave it a light squeeze. "We're not talking about them." She waited a moment, then spoke again. "What fun we used to have coming up here with Mimi when she was little."

"She loved it, crawling around the rocks and through the bushes."

"I'd get so panicky when she'd get too close to the edge."

"The logging chain you kept around her ankles would've kept her from falling."

She laughed.

"I haven't heard you laugh in a long time," I said, and tried pulling her closer. She sighed and kissed my cheek. "I think we ought to just stay here, take over that old cabin, and never go back into Greenfield, or the hospital, or the University."

She pointed to a cabin that had once belonged to Dutch and Mary Barnard, who had spent their summers there until age and infirmity became too limiting. A few years ago they donated it and the land to the Audubon Society, increasing its holdings at the Ledges.

"Bet the Audubon bureaucrats would kick us out the first night," I said.

"Poops."

"They'd probably say it was because their insurance policy wouldn't allow it."

"Poops," she said again. "Insurance people are even bigger poops. The worst kind of poops. When I was a little girl down in the mountains, if we got sick, we'd go to Doctor Hagaman. He'd charge three dollars for an office call, five dollars for a home call, and if you couldn't afford it, he'd take whatever you could pay, even if it was a basket of corn, a bunch of peas, greasy beans, whatever. He didn't worry about insurance. Once Daddy gave him a quart of his best corn liquor, and ever after, Dr. Hagaman said Daddy made the best corn in Watauga County."

"Think he carried malpractice?"

"Probably. We all do. But it wasn't the same in those days, not the practice of medicine, not the way the insurance companies run things, not anything." She was suddenly quiet. "How did that happen?"

"What?"

"It was beautiful, the sun, the view, and standing here with your arm on me was like being away on an island removed from turmoil and pain. And then bam, and we're back on the bad stuff. How did that happen, Tommy?"

"Insurance and malpractice."

"Damn," she said.

"There is no away." A hawk soared in close, a chipmunk struggling in its talons.

At Dutch and Mary's cabin, we sat on the porch, but it was shaded, and the spring air was cool once we were out of the sun. The flute player had stopped, and three five-year-old boys ran along the trail making loud shooting sounds as they pointed at each other with their fingers, followed by their parents, each with a can of beer, cigarettes dangling from their lips.

On our return walk to the trailhead, we stopped again at the rim of the Ledges, and gazed over the valley below. Silent cars and trucks moved along the Mohawk Trail, stretching through the valley like a line on a living map. Other than our breathing, there was not another human sound: no voices, no engines, not an ax chopping into wood, only the wind moving leaves on bushes and trees, the songs of birds and, a few feet away, a chipmunk rustling the underbrush. A few white puffy clouds scudded across the sky, casting fast-moving shadows over fields and woodlands.

"It's beautiful," Jan said, reaching for my hand. Our fingers twined together.

"It is, in spite of what we've done to the Earth."

"It's not all bad. What people have done, I mean. Look how lovely the patterns of the fields are, and the way the village sits on the bend of the river, like it was meant to be there. People have helped make Earth beautiful."

"We're fouling the nest."

"And feathering it, too."

"You're such a romantic," I said.

"So are you. That's why you get so cranky. If you weren't a romantic, you wouldn't think things should be perfect and rail against imperfection."

"That's idealism, not romanticism."

"Poop."

"Poop?"

"Poop poop poop."

"I suppose that's your final comment on the matter, Doctor."

"It is, Professor."

We stood there until the shadows grew long. With the first chill of evening, we walked up the rutted trail to the parking area at the edge of Patten Road. Ours was the only car remaining in the lot. The views along the gravel road as we headed homeward were as spectacular as those from the Ledges. I drove slowly, the evening light soft on the hills. The Southwest Residential Towers on the University campus, rising in the distance, were a reminder of my mundane life.

"A wonderful day, but there is no away," I said again.

Jan did not reply.

It was dark by the time we pulled into Greenfield.

"Hungry," I asked, as we passed the Friendly's by the I-91 / Route 2 rotary.

She started with a soft cry. "I was asleep. I'm wiped," she said. "I want to go home and pull the covers over my head."

"Not even a hot fudge sundae?"

"Not even that. Just home and bed."

Half an hour later, she was asleep. I sat on the front porch drinking a glass of Chianti and staring at moths circling in the cone of light streaming from the street lamp across from the house. No cars passed by. Tuckerman Court, like Nevada Street, leads nowhere. It is a block long with only twelve houses and a low-lying patch of woods at the end. What was once a carefully tended garden is now a mass of trees, brush, and weeds, their roots tearing flagstone walks apart. In its midst stood the remains of a gazebo covered with vines and falling into pieces of rotted wood.

I thought of the stark world Joseph had shown me in Springfield: narrow streets and weed-covered lots strewn with old tires and broken glass, a place of abuse and sorrow. I also thought of his belief that those of us living on the Tuckerman Courts of the world are safely removed from the life he knew, instead occupying a realm that is orderly, pleasant, and free from the pain and suffering of the world's Nevada Streets, those hopeless corridors not unlike the ones on which I had spent my childhood.

The trees, their leafy canopies high above our roofs, our manicured lots, our large, comfortable homes stoked a rage in him that I had felt all too violently. I may not feel the exact actuality of what he and his sister endured, but I am sure he knows nothing of the lives behind the walls and doors on streets such as ours, and how they can mirror his own, even if only in a minor key. Joseph's childhood world was one of misery, death, and abuse. But misery, death, and abuse exist on all streets.

Two doors up from our house, Edna Fulmer had kept her broken-bodied and retarded daughter, Ruth, locked in a room for twelve years, and would no doubt have kept her there longer had Edna not died of an aortic aneurysm. She lay dead in her living room for three days, undiscovered until Ruth's cries of hunger and despair reached a volume the neighborhood could not ignore. Then Garry Blackbird broke a window, crawled through into the house, and found her on the floor, the television remote still in her hand. Ruth was trapped in her bedroom, her covers in shreds from her attempts at cleaning herself and the bed of excrement.

People on the street still talk about the Johnson brothers, who killed their parents in the 1950s, took all the money and jewelry they could find, and drove their father's '54 Corvette to the Jersey Shore, only to get drunk and pile it into a telephone pole. They both died in the crash. That happened long before Jan and I moved to Tuckerman Court, but it is still part of the lore of the neighborhood, just like the messy divorce that resulted from Grace Simpson's affair with her next door neighbor's daughter, and Harvey Anderson's suicide, hanging himself from a sugar maple in the back yard, kicking over the aluminum ladder he had set up to reach the limb around which he had tied the rope.

It is as if Tuckerman Court has a memory of its own, a sense of place and continuity its residents share, one that becomes part of the consciousness of everyone who lives here. At our neighborhood black party last fall, even the newest couple—Jack and Harry Evans-Haynes, in their house for less than a year—participated in the conversation about the street's history with a striking sense of immediacy, as if they had been in residence during each occurrence.

Sitting on the porch, I watched the moths. They appeared to be in random motion, flitting and spiraling with no direction, no purpose, no predictability, yet never seeming to touch one another no matter how close they came, how intersecting their paths might be. I watched them for a long time.

Later, I sat in a chair in the living room and tried to read an article by Chomsky on anarchy. I gave up after five minutes, my head pounding. I have always been a reader and a writer. I subscribe to a number of scholarly journals and regularly read more in the department library. I keep up on the new books in my field, reading the most promising and at least skimming through as many of the others as I can.

Since losing my eye, reading has become difficult, tiring, my remaining eye strained and watery after less than an hour. Movies and television stress it as well. I've tried books on tape, but many of the things I need to read are obscure and available in recorded versions. Even if they were, I do not retain information I hear nearly as well as I do that I have read. The spoken word is impermanent; let loose upon the air, its sounds dissipate, scattering into nothingness. The written word is solid; I can return to it days, years after reading it and find it unchanged, except, perhaps, for my understanding of it.

Joseph and Randy robbed me of the ease with which I read. I put down the book, glad that Randy was dead and wishing Joseph the same fate. Active in antiwar movements, from Vietnam to Iraq, I have even withheld taxes in protest of the violence our government officials can promulgate, but I now looked hatred in the eye, and was appalled to find myself wishing death on a specific person. It's easy, when detestable politicians commit heinous acts, to say, "somebody ought take those assholes out behind the White House / State House / Capitol building / Town Hall and shoot them in the back of their heads." That's blowing off steam, and is not meant as a recipe for action. Setting the Chomsky down, I indulged my hatred, imagining doing slow, painful, and fatal damage to Joseph, pulling his toenails, breaking his fingers, hammering a nail into his right eye, saving the left eye for later, moving on to his tongue, ending forever his ability to excuse and explain himself.

The quiet broken only by the second hand of a quartz clock clicking each second, I reached over and turned off the light. The clicks suddenly seemed louder, the only light in the room coming from the streetlamp filtered through the window curtains. Through the stress-induced moisture and weakness of my functioning eye, long shadows of plants hanging from the window frames seemed to waver against the walls and over the floor.

"You bastard." I spoke into the dark, looking at a shadow that to my distorted vision resembled the shade of a man standing across the room. "You motherfucker," I said to it. "You piece of shit. You thief. You goddamn villain. You'll never be my friend. You are my enemy. If I ever have the chance I will kill you."

A car came up the street, its headlights through the windows causing the shadow to move like that of someone crossing the room to attack me. The car passed, and the shadow returned to its original position.

I turned on the television. It had been tuned to CNN, and Larry King was interviewing a blonde woman, her hair thick with mousse, and a thin man, his head shaved, his face in a scowl, asking questions at best peripheral to the upcoming Presidential election. The camera pulled away, and King faded, replaced by an announcement urging viewers to stay tuned for the second half of the show, which would feature a discussion about whether or not there was a continuing and secret tradition of plural marriage in mainstream Mormonism, and the effects of the disclosure of widespread child abuse in the recent bust of fundamentalist Latter Day Saints in Texas.

"What does this mean for Mitt Romney's hope that John McCain will select him as his running mate," the announcer asked.

"And what does it mean for the next twenty minutes, until there's another unpredictable non-event that you'll claim has national and international political importance?" I yelled at the set, clicking King away, clicking the Red Sox away, clicking until I once again found a M*A*S*H re-run and eased myself more comfortably into the chair. Content to fall asleep to its critique of the long ago Vietnam War disguised as a critique of the longer ago Korean War, I let the present slip away.

I awoke to a warm and sunny spring day, cardinals singing from the arbor vitae, squirrels digging in the garden looking for nuts. The smell of frying bacon filled the house as I went downstairs and walked into the kitchen. Jan sat at the table reading *The Recorder* and drinking coffee.

"Good morning," I said.

"Hey." She put down the paper and smiled up at me, her look and tone that of a person with no worries. "Sleep well?"

I almost told her the truth, but said, "Like a log."

"Me too. Must've been all that fresh air and hiking yesterday."

"Must've been. Anything interesting in the paper?"

"Same old stuff, school committee slugging it out with the mayor and the town council, more people dead in Iraq, dog licenses up for renewal in Northfield, the Democrats in disarray, the Republicans saying God's in his Heaven and all's right with the world."

"God being in his Heaven wouldn't necessarily make the world all right."

"I think he leaves the world alone so we can figure things out on our own. Coffee's ready and there's bacon and fries on the stove. You'll have to do your own eggs."

"Have you thought about retirement, Tom?"

R.C. Alexander, Chair of the Political Science department, had come to my office shortly after I arrived. Perching on the edge of my desk, he played with his pen and studied a print on the wall entitled "Marx and Lennon," with red silk screen images of Groucho Marx and John Lennon. It was the first time he had visited my office in more than a decade. We were colleagues only by virtue of teaching in the same department. We had never been friends, never sought each other out, our interchanges limited to those occurring at department meetings or chance passings in the corridors.

"I've got three more years before I can collect my full pension. Why?"

"Rumor is that the Legislature's going to do another five and five that'll let you add any combination adding up to five years to your time in service and age. That might let you bail."

For the briefest of moments, I indulged the thought of how I was finding myself increasingly dismayed, a cynical and jaded liberal, weary beyond caring. Was I ready to retire from the University and walk away from my lifelong field of study? Did I want to cancel my journals? Was I ready to turn to the sports and comics pages in the newspapers and ignore the front pages, editorial and op-ed sections, ready to restrict myself to the daily local news rag and never open the *New York Times* again? Would I be satisfied to prop myself up on the couch and watch morning TV, cable news outlets, Monday night football, and the endless series of forensic detective and police dramas on the other evenings?

"You going to take it, R.C.?"

"No way. What would I do if I retired? Nah, they'll have to carry me out feet first."

"You think I'd do any better?"

He put the pencil down and swung around to look at me. "You've become a curmudgeon. You're cranky about and to your students, you undermine the discipline of our field with your screwball ideas about its validity. You act as though you don't like anybody in the department and, quite frankly, no one particularly cares for you. When's the last time you gave a party or were invited to one?"

"I don't like you," I said, the words exploding unexpectedly, true but never before spoken. It was as if a spider had run across my brain, tickling the truth from its deep hiding places. "I never did. You're a poor administrator and you've got an over-inflated idea of the department's importance. Whether you like it or not, I'm important here. Someone has to teach the politics of chaos."

He straightened his back and fashioned a smile that reminded me of a dog baring its teeth. "There've been some complaints from the School of Education that you hold their graduate students who take your courses to the same standards as our own."

"I do."

"Bad interdepartmental politics. Education students are different."

"What's this all about, R.C.?"

"You know Wiley Simmons, right?"

"The state senator."

"You probably know he's chair of the Senate Finance Committee."

"I tend to be aware of political positions and the people who hold them."

He ignored me. "He sits on the Education Committee, and his son's graduating from Penn this year with a Ph.D. in contemporary Chinese political thought. It would be a coup to get him in this department, for a number of reasons."

"And this has what to do with me?"

"There are no openings. Somebody has to leave in order to create one."

"Me?"

"It's logical."

"You'd have to conduct a nationwide search to fill my position, assuming, of course, that I'd be willing to retire, which I'm not. How would the Simmons kid stand up against such a pool?"

He spread his arms. "There are searches and there are searches. We can hire almost anybody we want if the right people are on the search committee and the right job description and the right qualifications are posted."

"Speaking of right things, this isn't the right time for me to go." I stood up, took his elbow, and eased him off my desk and toward the door. "It is the right time for you to leave my office."

"Think about it. You'd have all the free time in the world and a hefty state pension to finance you, plus whatever that rich doctor wife of yours brings in." He looked at his hands, flexed his fingers, and then looked back up at me. "You're not what you used to be. Your student evaluations say you sometimes ramble and seem to be making things up. You really do need to think about retiring."

"I've thought. See you at the next department meeting, R.C."

"You're not getting any younger," he said.

"And you're still a master of cliché and stale thinking."

His eyes flashed, and I could see him making a huge effort to restrain himself. "I can't believe you'd turn down an opportunity like this. We all thought you'd jump at the chance."

"What do you mean 'we all'?"

He flushed. "I was speaking metaphorically. I really meant me."

"It wasn't a metaphor. You said you all thought I'd take an early retirement. This is a department request, not one just from you."

"Forget it. I misspoke."

"I guess I'm just not predictable."

"No. What you are, Rutherford, is a fool. I can make life miserable for you: teaching assignments, hours, committees, advising."

I laughed. "Have you read the collective bargaining contract lately?"

He glared at me. "That's just words, and words can be interpreted in many ways."

"Fiction and poetry, maybe, but contracts are pretty specific."

When he shut the door behind him, it was just short of a slam.

Alone, I thought about retirement. R.C. was right in his description of my relationship to work and my colleagues. Jan and I could both afford to retire, and if we did, we could travel, and I could continue my research and writing scholarly articles. Best of all, I'd be free of academic politics and concerns. It was a pleasant thought, but I would never give R.C. the satisfaction of leaving. It would be irrational, against my best interests, to stay if the Legislature did offer a five and five plan, but people behave in strange and unpredictable ways.

As R.C. was attempting to encourage my retirement, Jan went to her office following rounds at the hospital.

"My patients were doing well," she told me that evening before we went to bed. "There were no emergencies and no births. The nursery had three babies I'd helped deliver the day before, and they were all healthy, kicking and crying and doing what babies are supposed to do. It was a warm and beautiful day, and I thought I had an easy day ahead. All my office patients were in the early stages of pregnancy and only needed routine checkups and my assurance that everything was fine."

"Sounds like the ideal day."

"Until eleven o'clock, when I had a call from Ed Riley."

"The new chief of staff at the hospital," I asked.

She nodded. "Charles Mathews went to see him today."

I motioned for her to go on.

"He told me that Mathews filed a formal complaint against the hospital, and wrongful death charges and a malpractice suit against me. Seems like he's covering every base."

I nodded.

"'He can't touch me,' I said, but Riley told me Mathews has called a press conference for five this afternoon, just in time to make the evening newscasts. I didn't understand why the press would be interested in him, but Riley said 'It's a big story for a little town like Greenfield. This could be very bad for us.'"

"He meant the hospital, not you, right?"

"I asked him that. He said 'I'm troubled by what it could mean for you.'"

"But he's scared shitless about what it would mean for the hospital," I said to her.

"Exactly," she said. "And then he wished me good luck and hung up."

"I'm sorry," I said.

She shrugged. "I'm free, Tommy. Jesus has done that for me, lifted my burdens and made me realize that nothing can touch me, just like I told Ed."

"You told him that?"

"I said Jesus has set me free, and nothing he can do or say can touch me."

"Nothing?"

"Nothing."

"I'm not sure that was a good thing to say."

"It's wonderful, Tommy. Jesus has insulated me from the pain of existence."

"And the joys?"

"He is the joy."

"And Miriam? Me?"

"The joy I get from you both is within the joy Jesus provides."

"You mean we're secondary."

"Jesus will be with me throughout eternity. You and Miriam are of the earth, and the earth will fade away. Unless, of course, we are blessed enough to meet again on the golden shore." Her voice was soft, without inflection. It made me think of the voices of the women in the fundamentalist Mormon sect that had been raided by the police. Her vibrancy and intensity were gone; in their place was an affect like that of someone drugged.

"You believe in golden shores and the ever-after?"

"I don't know, Tommy. All I know is that Jesus sustains me. What is planned for us after this life is a mystery. He spoke of his father's kingdom, but you know as well as I do that theologians and priests and scholars have been arguing for two thousand years over what that means, whether it's an actual place, a state of being, or a bit of grace we achieve in the few short years we have. The only thing no one who has experienced Jesus' presence argues about is that it's life-changing. Nothing can be the same once Jesus has entered your heart."

I sighed. "I don't know what to say."

She took my hand and held it to her cheek. "You don't have to say anything, Tommy. Just be happy for me."

"I feel like I'm losing you."

"You could be gaining Jesus. He could save us both from the world."

"I rather like the world," I said.

"With people like those men in it?"

"Joseph and Randy?"

"They did a horrible thing to you."

"I didn't say the world was all good, just that I like living in it."

She patted my cheek and removed her hand. "I like it better now that Jesus protects me."

My sleep that night was filled with torturous and fractured images of violence, Joseph lying before me, battered and dead. When I awoke in the morning, I was tired, my arms and back aching, but strangely elated by the content of my dreams.

Seven

Joseph was waiting for me the next morning at eight when I stopped by Greenfield's Market, a health food store in downtown Greenfield, to get my coffee for the morning ride to Amherst.

"Good morning, old boy. Bloody awful news conference that Mathews chap put on last night, wasn't it?"

"You're a Brit now?"

"Haven't I always been?"

"What about growing up in Springfield?"

He laughed. "Oh, that."

"It was all a lie? Nevada Street, your sister, the foster homes and abuse?"

"It's not worth discussing. I'm more concerned about your wife's situation."

I brushed past him into the market.

"I'd like to help," he said, standing beside me as I filled my travel mug with Rattlesnake Morning Brew.

"I don't need your help."

"Your wife does, doesn't she? And the wife of my friend is my friend. By the way, old chap," he added, "your daughter is having a problem with a music teacher at Watauga County High. He's been following her home and parking outside her apartment for hours at a time. From what I understand, she is quite rattled by him. The daughter of my friend is also my friend."

I froze. "How would you know about that, and why hasn't Mimi told me?"

He suddenly spoke with an exaggerated mountain dialect. "Listen good buddy, I got friends everywhere. Y'awl didn't reckon you were my only one, did you? I might could arrange some he'p for that little girl of your'un. It might could be she don't want to upset you. Y'awl got enough on your plate, and she figgered you ain't got no dog in this fight."

"I'll talk to her. You just keep out of it."

"What about Johnny Shook," he asked, as we walked toward the checkout line.

I handed the cashier the correct change. "Johnny Shook?"

"He's the music teacher."

"I'm not going to discuss my problems with you."

"So he is a problem." He rested his hand on my shoulder, and walked beside me as I left the store.

"That's not what I meant."

"But that's what you said."

I pulled away from him. "Leave me alone, leave my family alone, and leave my problems alone." I got in the car and closed the door, pulling away as he stood on the curb smiling, waving with his fingers.

I called Miriam on my cell phone as I drove along the River Road.

"Hi Daddy," she said. "What's wrong?"

"I was going to ask you the same thing."

She hesitated before replying. "Why?"

"You having problems at work?"

"Everything's fine," she said, too quickly.

"Nobody bothering you?"

I heard her take a deep breath. "Why would you ask that, Daddy? Who's been talking to you?"

"A father always wonders about such things."

"Bullshit, Daddy. Somebody told you something."

"About the teacher who's stalking you? You're right, somebody did talk to me, and said you were worried. Now I'm worried."

"He's not stalking. He's just infatuated, and I'm not interested in him. Sometimes he'll just stand under my window looking hangdog and sing my name. It's sad, really. Who told you?"

"Nobody you know."

"Bullshit again, Daddy. You're the one that doesn't know anybody down here, so someone down here must have been worried about me and figured out how to get in touch with you. That pisses me off, Daddy. I can take care of myself, and I'd like to know who down here is interfering with my right to do that."

"Doesn't it worry you that this guy might be so out of touch that he doesn't realize it's inappropriate to follow you around and stand under your window crooning? Who knows what he might do? You should call the cops."

"Right. And lose my job. His name's Johnny Shook. His daddy's a deputy sheriff and his mother's on the school board. He lives alone in a log house in Valle Crucis that he rebuilt and renovated. He gave a party last Christmastime for everybody in the school who'd come. Only eight of us did. When I raved about the place and the beautiful work he'd done on it, he took it the wrong way and thought I was sweet on him."

"Men like that can be dangerous."

She chuckled. "Not Johnny. He's just kind of sad. He's bright and sweet and slightly out of phase with the rest of the world, but he's a good musician, and he somehow gets the kids excited about music." She paused for a moment, then added, "I think he may have Asperger's Syndrome. He teaches a night class at the local community college, on economic theory in the world of Donald Duck and Scrooge McDuck. Now that's a little strange, right quirky, screwy really, like some of the Trekkies and their ilk, but how harmful can a man be who's totally into duck comics and teaching music?"

"I think that makes him even scarier."

"How'd you hear about this?"

"From a friend."

"And how come you have a friend who knows what's going on in Boone?"

"That's not the point, Mimi."

"It's my point, Daddy. It's a lot weirder than having Johnny Shook follow me around, like you have a secret spy ring checking up on me."

She was right. If I didn't tell her the full story, she could end up thinking someone besides Shook was stalking her.

"It was Joseph," I said.

"One of the men who beat you? How could he know about this, and why would he tell you, and why would you listen to him?"

"He says he's decided to be my friend, and that he has friends all over the world, including one in North Carolina who told him about this Johnny Shook."

"And you're worried about me? Daddy, you've got to go to the police before he does something worse to you."

"I did. They're working on it." I didn't tell her the Greenfield Police Department was so underfunded and overworked that it was up to me to watch out for Joseph and cover my back. "Do you want help?"

"I'm all right."

"I can come down."

"No, Daddy." She nearly yelled the words into the phone. "I can handle this. Johnny's not a threat, just an embarrassment."

"I worry," I said.

"I understand, but I'm all right. I'll let you know if there are any problems."

There was nothing more I could say, and it was clear she would not abide my showing up in Boone. We hung up just as I reached the Route 116 exit to the University.

As I had no classes, and there was nothing on my schedule until an eleven o'clock curriculum committee meeting, I walked around campus, wandering without purpose over the grass, ignoring paths and buildings. The air was clear and warm, the sky cloudless. Small clusters of students sat under trees and leaned against walls, smoking and laughing. Some were studying, but most seemed more interested in one another than in books and preparations for the final exams that were a week or two away. Others wandered around as aimlessly as I, their eyes blank and their faces expressionless. They could be pondering the fate of the universe, planning a pizza order, or emptying their minds of everything but contemplation of the air... or stoned out of their minds.

A boy tossed a Frisbee to another standing by a tree to my left. I watched as it soared over the lawn, my two dimensional vision failing to warn me that it was coming too close to my head. It glanced off my ear and landed at my feet. I picked it up and tossed it back, rubbing my sore ear and angry at Joseph for leaving me so vulnerable.

A young woman wearing a light cotton summer dress sat on a wall. Her hair hung long over her shoulders as she looked into the eyes of a boy serenading her in a high voice, accompanying his song on a guitar the size of a dulcimer. His bare arms were covered with tattoos, and lightning tattoos were on either side of his shaven head. A mass of earrings hung from his lobes, and he had a nose stud that glittered in the sunlight. It was a common and harmless campus scene, young people caught up in the fashions of their times, courting as the young will always do. They reminded me of our fads in the Sixties, designed in the same defiance of parental expectations and tastes.

One of the best parts of working at the University was the tolerance of youthful styles I had learned, seeing the same vulnerable and questing minds behind it as I had known in the acid-tripping, bell-bottomed-and-torn-dungaree, tie-died, long-haired, dope- smoking, building-occupying, cop-baiting behaviors of my own youth. Styles have changed dramatically, but the guitars and serenades remain unchanged. I thought of lines from Yeats that I had memorized as an undergraduate.

Fish, flesh, or fowl, commend all summer long
Whatever is begotten, born, and dies.
Caught in that sensual music all neglect
Monuments of unageing intellect.

I understood them anew for the first time.

Wondering if her parents would have a like tolerance, or if they would react with alarm, could they see that boy so ardently courting their daughter, I suddenly imagined my daughter pursued by a mildly autistic man, frightened as she sat in her room behind drawn curtains and shades, he standing below, moonlight streaming over him, reflected in his eyes as he looked up at her shadow on the curtains and softly sang her name. Did he for a moment believe she might throw those curtains back, open the window, and lean out to hear his song, looking down upon him with a loving gaze? Did he have a gun tucked into his belt that he was prepared to empty into her should she continue to ignore his attentions? Things like that happen, senseless acts of violence that forever change the lives of their victims or, in the most tragic instances, those of their survivors.

Who better than I to understand how one can suffer from the capricious and malign will of others? I reached for my phone to call her back, thought better of it, and stopped as soon as I had entered the area code on the keypad. I was too distant to protect her, and she would not forgive me should I appear in Boone to act as her defender.

On an impulse, I sat on a wall opposite from where the young woman was being serenaded. My phone still in hand, I clicked on the calls received menu. Scrolling down until I found the only unfamiliar number listed, I pressed *Call*. Joseph picked up after two rings, still speaking in his idea of a mountain dialect.

"Hey there, good buddy. Where are you?"

"Why does it matter?"

"I like to know where I'm talking to, just like I want to know who I'm talking to."

"I'm at the University," I said.

"See, now did that cost you anything to say?"

I said nothing.

"How y'awl doing, Thomas?"

"Finding my way in a two-dimensional world, thanks to you."

"That shouldn't be no problem for someone at a university, good buddy. Shee-it, maybe me and Randy he'ped you fit in better."

"I talked to Miriam. You were right about that man following her around."

"Did y'awl doubt me?"

"You said you had a friend down there."

"Roby Ward, I think his name is. Or Howard Triplett. Maybe it's Bobby Joe Rominger, Kenny Lee Byrd, Jack Ward, something like that. Hell, I don't rightly know. Maybe I knowed him from when I was in Vietnam."

"You're not old enough to have been in Vietnam."

"You might could be right on that, buddy. I knowed him from somewhere though. Maybe that Gulf War, or somthin'. Little thangs like that have a way of slipping out of my head, you know? Why y'awl asking?"

"I'll call you back," I said, having second thoughts about contacting him.

"Anytime, dear friend." The line went dead.

My heart racing, my breath quick and unsettled, I couldn't allow myself to think about what it would mean should I ask Joseph for help, what I would be opening myself to from him.

"Fuck it," I said aloud, and pressed redial. I'd obviously spoken with more intensity and volume than I'd intended, for the boy stopped playing, and both he and the girl looked at me and smiled. The boy gave me a thumbs up.

"Cool, man," he said, and returned to his playing.

I redialed. Joseph answered before the first ring ended, "What do you need?"

"Your friend, can he check on Miriam from time to time?"

"I reckon he's already doing that, good buddy."

"And he can see to it that she'll be all right?"

"You ain't got a thang to worry about, Thomas."

"Good." I snapped the phone shut before I had to thank him.

Clouds moved in quickly. By 10:30 the sky was gray and threatening. Thunder rumbled over the valley, and streaks of lightning ripped the sky. The weatherman the night before on Channel 40 had predicted a warm, sunny day, with possible light showers by midnight. It started to rain before noon, and by 1:30, limited visibility and a steady and heavy downpour had closed the day in with a damp, chilly bleakness.

The meeting was uncomfortable. R.C. chaired the curriculum committee, and he wanted to be sure that the newly hired Chancellor—a political scientist who had taught with distinction at Georgetown, Chapel Hill, and Ann Arbor before becoming an administrator—would view us as an organized and forward looking department, a model for the future of the science, in his words. I sat and listened, but added nothing to the discussion as my colleagues, many as old as I, put forth theories and positions they had been promulgating for as long as I had been in the department.

I doodled for a while, drawing unflattering caricatures of them, and wondering why I was determined to stay working there, and how seriously R.C. would labor to get me into retirement, and what kind of loss of identity I would suffer after leaving the University, whether of my own accord or as the result of the subtle pressures unfriendly administrators have the resources to exert.

My mind drifted to other losses: my eye and the three-dimensional world to Joseph and Randy's mindless assault; Jan to Jesus; my integrity to Joseph because I had asked him for help, presuming on his unwanted and unwarranted declaration of friendship; and now my fears about Mimi's safety. Engulfed in uncertainty and fear, I forced myself to cough repeatedly, using it as an excuse to leave the meeting.

I went to my office. Shutting the door, I folded my arms on the desk and rested my head on them. Rain beat against the window. My heart pounded. My ruined eye ached. My mind raced over a collage of disjointed thoughts and images, emotions that would rise and disappear in no order, with no reason I could determine. I stood and waved my arms to chase them away, and was overcome with vertigo and nausea. I looked at the window to see the gray, rainy day it kept out, and suddenly it glowed with a pulsating white glow that was filled with tiny dark spaces, like a luminous piece of Swiss cheese, the spaces moving rapidly, colliding and bouncing away, only to collide with another, their sizes and shapes shifting. The glow was frightening, more like a visual pain than light, a scream translated from the audible to the visible spectrum. My mouth was heavy with the taste of bile, and I fell over, watching helplessly as the edge of the desk rose toward my forehead.

I awoke on a narrow cot in a strange room, windowless, with a powerful light suspended from the ceiling shining in my eyes, like those in operating rooms. The walls were painted a gelato yellow, and each had a closed doorway. My head pounded, and my right ear was ringing. A man leaned over me and snapped his fingers by my right ear, then my left. I could barely hear the second attempt. Putting his lips by my right ear, he spoke.

"*Monsieur, êtes-vous en douleur?*" He spoke with a Parisian accent, although his use of words was awkward, as if he were translating mechanically from English as he thought.

I looked at him, the light blurring my eye. I rubbed it several times, and it cleared enough for me to see Joseph's face close to mine. He wore a beret, and had used eyebrow liner or something similar to draw a pencil-thin mustache on his upper lip.

"I'm fine, just a little sore and disoriented, but not really in pain." I replied to his question in English. "You're Parisian today?"

"*Je suis beaucoup d'hommes.*"

"You're many men?"

"*Oui. Je suis une horde.*" He spread his arms wide and laughed.

"You're a fucking crazy bastard."

Putting a forefinger to his lips he smiled and shook his head. "*Non non non.*"

"And how did you know I speak French?" I had written my dissertation on the effect of the Reign of Terror on political philosophy, a study in chaos and loss of reason. It earned me my Ph.D., and the enmity of most of the faculty I had studied with, undermining as it did their beliefs in the science of the political order. It had been buried in the archives at the university almost as soon as I tore the last sheet from the typewriter. With my advisor long dead, and most of the faculty members who worked with me also in the grave or retired, I thought no one knew about it.

"*Ah, Monsieur, je sais tous vos secrets foncés, vos grands accomplissements, vos amours, vos haines, vos indifferences.*"

"I have no dark secrets, and no great accomplishments. My hates and loves have always been obvious. For example, I despise those who use the French language carelessly. Speak English."

He laughed again. "*Certainement. Une forme spécifique? J'ai une légion de dialects.*"

"Whatever. Just use English and tell me how I got here, and where here is."

He bowed from the waist and swept his beret through the air. "Very well, Monsieur. I came by your office two hours ago and found that you had—how do you Americans put it?—knocked yourself out somehow." He stroked my forehead. His hands were calloused and rough. "Several of your colleagues were milling about. One said he had just come in to borrow a book and found you there. They were debating about calling an ambulance, but I told them I was your friend, *votre ami*, and said I would take care of you. They helped me get you to my car, and I brought you here."

"Where am I?"

"Can you hear me well?" He snapped his fingers again over each ear.

I pointed to the right one. "Sounds like it's stuffed with cotton. Where am I?"

"My bunker. I can take you home if you wish."

"I wish. And I want you to stay out of my life."

"And your daughter's?"

"And hers."

He smiled. "Too late, friend. You asked me to intervene."

"I asked you to have someone keep an eye on her, and I shouldn't have done that."

"She's fine, you know. The creep isn't bothering her anymore."

"You're sure of that? And how?"

He wiped the back of his hand over his upper lip three times, and when he took it away, the thin mustache was gone. Pulling in his chin and hunching his shoulders, his face seemed to change, and when he spoke again, it was in a deep voice with what sounded like a northern Mississippi drawl, as if I were listening to Orson Welles playing Will Varner talking to Paul Newman as Ben Quick, the cleaned-up Flem Snopes in *The Long Hot Summer*, Martin Ritt's bastardized version of Faulkner's "The Long Summer" portion of *The Hamlet*.

"There's men, you know," he half mumbled, "that want sumpin' so bad they'll do almost anything to get it. It might be a woman, or it might be a horse, a good huntin' dog with a cry you can hear and recognize two miles away; it might be land, or a big white house where folks come from all over the world to kiss their asses and ask for money, or weapons, or beg them not to go to war with them but with somebody else, or it might could be nothin' more than finding somebody smaller'n them to whup so they can feel bigger than they are, or at least act like they do. It don't matter a hell of a lot what it is, as long as it's sumpin' they want so bad that just thinkin' about it makes 'em tremble, burns in 'em so fierce that if they touch a finger to somebody's barn, it'll burst into flames that break through the roof before anybody knows the spark's been lit, and not stop till there's nothin' more'n a cold pile of ashes and horse bones and cow bones, and maybe the bones of some poor son-of-a-bitch stable-hand that couldn't get out of the ragin' inferno that come off the end of their finger. They got that kind of heat in 'em and it don't never cool down. They could go swimmin' in the Antarctic to cool, and all they'd end up accomplishin' would be to singe the feathers off'n some of them poor penguins they got down there and maybe evaporating enough ice to raise the ocean levels another fraction of an inch. I've not figgered out what it is you want, friend. Sometimes it seems like little things, such as knowin' that girl of yours is safe and secure, and sometimes it seems like you got a vision of how things ought to be, and you want other folks to look at that vision and say 'my god, ain't that a grand vision. Why didn't I think of it? Goddamn, but I got to tell everybody I know about it so the world can change.'"

He took a cigar from his pocket, bit the end off, and put whole thing in his mouth. Wetting it completely down, he touched a match to one end and sucked on the other until the lit end was glowing with a brightness that almost hurt my eye.

"Now, what you got to say for yo'se'f, friend?"

"Who in the hell... what in the hell are you?"

He took a long drag on the cigar and let the smoke out slowly, most of it through his mouth, but a thin stream came from his nostrils. "I thought I told you that, friend. The name's Joseph."

"Joseph who?"

He shrugged. "That depends on the day and the time of the day. Today, I reckon you could call me Joseph Ratliff. Could be Jones, or Smith, or Collins, or Kowalski, Conrad, or just plain Joseph with no last name. Then again, it could be anywhere between three and six thousand names. It don't matter what you call me, as long as you call me friend."

I sat up, my head swimming. "You are fucking crazy."

He smiled. "You've said that before, at least once, and I suppose I am, but you're the one lying in my bunker."

"Take me back to the University, so I can get my car and go home." I was trying not to shake.

"That what you want?"

I nodded.

He held out an arm. "Let me he'p you up."

I wrenched away from him. "I can do it myself."

"I suppose you can. The question is, should you?"

I pushed myself from the cot and stood. A moment later, my head was spinning, and Joseph was holding me in his arms.

"Careful," he said, the drawl was gone, replaced by a speech pattern similar to my own. "Steady yourself on the cot, and take a deep breath."

I braced myself, and took several long, deep breaths. Slowly I felt stronger, clearer, and I rose, standing alone.

"You all right," he asked.

"I think so."

He pointed to the door on the farthest wall from my cot. "Through there, but don't move too fast. You might faint again."

Leading the way, he opened the door through which I could see a narrow staircase. "Up there." He stood aside to let me pass and followed close behind, his hand on my back to keep me from falling backwards toward him. "There's a trap door at the top. Push it up."

I did, and scrambled out on the ground to find myself in a heavily wooded area, a narrow path leading through the underbrush to my left. Joseph was behind me. "I'll have to blindfold you. I wouldn't want you returning uninvited, and I certainly wouldn't want you bringing anybody else here."

"Like the police," I said.

"Like them, friend." He took a blue bandana with a white pattern from his pocket. "Let me tie this on."

I didn't protest, and a moment later I could see nothing.

"You disappoint me, Thomas." He put a hand on my shoulder and gently pushed me along, warning me of trees, roots, rocks, and uneven places in the path that I could trip on were I not aware of them.

"How's that?"

"You don't ask enough questions, and you're far too passive in this situation."

"You don't answer the ones I do ask."

"That's because you don't ask the right ones."

"Perhaps I'm passive because I don't have any precedent for a situation like this."

"Lots of men would've gotten a gun after being beaten as badly as Randy and I beat you."

"I have guns. A Smith and Wesson .22 on a .38 Police Special frame, a 1937 Marlin .22 rifle, and a single shot Winchester 12 gauge shotgun."

He laughed. "You could have taken me out any time you wanted with any of them. You got .22 hollow points?"

I nodded.

"Ouch. Why didn't you shoot me?"

I had no answer. We walked with his hand on my shoulder, only his directions guiding me through the wilderness to break the silence. There were no other sounds except those of our feet as we cracked twigs and rustled leaves. Even with the blindfold, I could tell when we left the woods. The light coming through the material brightened, and the ground surface evened out.

"The car's about five steps ahead," he said. "Reach out your left arm, walk slowly, and you'll touch it in a moment. I'll open the door and I'll help you to get in. I'll remove the blindfold when we're far enough away that you won't see any landmarks that'll lead you back here."

"Is that your home, the bunker?"

He laughed. "No. I've got an old farmhouse in southern New Hampshire."

"Family?" My only purpose in asking the question was in hope of finding a human strain in him, something that would render him normal, a person whose needs might somehow match my own. Even as I asked, I knew it was futile. He surprised me in a fashion.

"Cats. Twelve of them." We reached the car. Opening the door, he helped me in. "They don't need me. When I'm gone, I let them out, and they take care of themselves. As soon as I come home, they begin to filter back into the house, and if I'm there for a week they're all inside."

He shut the door, and I heard the sound of his footsteps as he walked around the car. The door opened and he got in the driver's side. I felt his heat as he brushed my chest, reaching across me to open the glove compartment. After a brief a rustling of papers and small objects, he closed it with a click and moved away. There were several moments of silence as he did something, and then he reached across again, opened the compartment, and dropped whatever he had taken out back in. After another minute or two, he started the car, and we began moving.

Twenty minutes later, he stopped and removed the blindfold. We were on the side of Route 116, about thirty feet west of the I-91 Deerfield/Conway interchange. Joseph was again wearing the pencil line mustache and his beret.

"*Monsieur*," he said, "*comment-allez vous?*"

"*Tres bien*," I sighed.

"*Bon. Bon.*" He put the car in gear, and we drove back to the University parking lot without talking. Pulling next to my car, he shut off his ignition and half turned in his seat to face me.

"You're still not asking questions, let alone the right ones."

"What didn't I ask?"

He smiled and shook his head in a slow and deliberate manner. "You never asked why I took you to my bunker."

"I'll play your game. Why did you take me to your bunker?"

"Aside from the fact that I couldn't leave you at the office in the condition you were in, I wanted you to see it."

"Why?"

"Not a probing question, but a natural one. I wanted you to understand how organized I am. You've seen but one room of an underground complex that could house a large group of people for a long period of time."

"How large a group and for how long?"

"Obvious questions, given what I just said."

"What does the bunker mean to you?"

"Ah, *monsieur*, a better question. It represents unknown worlds. Most people walking through those woods would never notice anything. The more perceptive among them might notice an irregularity in the forest floor, but think nothing of it once they had passed by. Few are those, and there have not yet been any, who would examine the location carefully enough to wonder about it. None, I dare say, would find the bunker."

"What does that have to do with unknown worlds?"

"It is a small world unto itself. Free from the grid, it nonetheless has power, running water, heat, all the amenities of civilization, yet no one but you and I know of it. Randy did, of course, but the poor soul is no longer with us."

"Because you killed him."

He removed the beret and used it to wipe the mustache from his upper lip. Then he leaned toward me, speaking in a rough imitation of film noir Bogart. "Lissen pal, I never copped to that, and I never will. The poor sap's dead, yeah, but I didn't have nothin' to do with it."

"Then who killed him?"

"You?"

"Don't be ridiculous. I've never killed anyone."

"You sure of that? Like I told you earlier, killing someone's a terrible thing to do. If I'd've done it, I wouldn't remember it, couldn't remember it. Maybe it's like that with you. Didn't you want him dead? Didn't you ever think about killing him?"

"And you. I thought about how good it would feel to kill you both after the beating you gave me, after this eye." I pointed to the patch over my empty socket.

"Maybe you done it to him, killed the mug 'cause of what he done to you, and then you put it out of your mind so it wouldn't bother you; so you wouldn't wake up in the middle of the night with his dead face staring down at you in the dark, glowing like a jack-o'-lantern and pointing a bony finger at you and saying how you killed him. Maybe you just willed yourself to forget, friend, how his eyes looked when he knew he was going to die, and that yours was the last face he'd see on this earth."

"And maybe those are your memories," I said.

"I got no memories, pal. I just got the moment."

"No one's got just the moment. We all extend into the past."

"And into the future," he asked. "Does the future exist?"

"Not in my book."

"Where will you be in ten seconds?"

"Probably right here."

"See. The future."

"I've got to go," I said.

"Where?"

"Home."

"You'll be home soon?"

"With luck."

"The future, if you're lucky, you say. Something could come along and change the future or prevent it."

"You can't prevent what hasn't happened."

"Yeah? Suppose somebody's got a gun to your head and is going to pull the trigger and somebody else comes up behind him and caps him before he can cap you. Ain't that changing the future, pal?"

"This is pointless."

"My point, exactly. It don't do you no good to remember the past or think about the future."

Resting my hand on the door handle, I said, "Why does the bunker represent unknown worlds?"

"Did I say that it did?"

"You did."

"What a goddamn dumb thing for me to say. Lissen, pal, sometimes I say things to impress people. I suppose that was one of those times."

I opened the door and climbed free of the car. "Don't come around any more," I said, and closed it behind me.

He smiled, waved, and, putting the car in reverse, spun out of the parking lot. I heard his wheels squeal as he hit the street, his engine roaring.

Eight

Driving home, I emptied my mind as I passed the sod farm on River Road. I drove past the small houses and mobile homes next to it, and the farms farther along. Ignoring the shortcut over the hills to Routes 5 & 10, I continued along the river, passing more old farms, their soil rich and black from endless ages of flooding and silt deposit. Dotted with newer homes on lots farmers had sold off over the years in order to make ends meet, the road rose above the flood plain and ran through an area of ledge covered with pines and hardwood, houses set in their dark reaches, then it descended again onto the flood plain with its flat, rich farm land. A small cemetery sat in the middle of the fields to my right. Surrounded by a white picket fence, marked with a home-made sign, "Pine Nook Cemetery", it looked almost inviting. Gravel tracks ran through the fields down toward the Connecticut River, some farm lanes, others leading to long abandoned ferry landings.

Less than a mile past the cemetery, River Road makes a sharp left turn a few feet in front of a brown frame house that would be in the middle of the road if the right-of-way continued straight ahead. A car had missed the turn and was sitting on the porch, halfway in the front door. A small group of men and women and two children stood around the car, looking at the damage and scratching their heads, pointing at each other and speaking in voices loud enough for me to hear in my closed car, but mixed into an angry, indistinguishable babble.

I took the turn and drove uphill toward Greenfield. The scenery gave way to hardscrabble houses, fields covered with scrub growth and old machinery. To my left was the entrance to a rural automobile junkyard, and a little farther on the right, I was looking down on the East Deerfield freight yards: miles of railroad track and hundreds of box cars filling the air with squealing brakes, clacking wheels on steel rails, the loud clank and hiss of shuttle engines moving the cars from place to place, rattling and banging against one another as they were hitched and unhitched.

I was amazed at how the railroad people managed to create and maintain order with the multitude of cars and goods scattered over the huge yard, wondering what manner of software and hardware they could use to organize what appeared to be a tangled mass of rails, cars, and engines moving amid the din. We humans are creatures of disorder desperately trying to create the appearance of order. Nature may abhor a vacuum, but humanity both abhors and adores order. We are driven to create it and destroy it.

Crossing the Green River into Greenfield, I pulled myself back to practicality. I had to do something. Joseph was correct; I had been passive, and if that disappointed him, it distressed me. Worse, I didn't know what questions I should ask; not of him, not of myself, not of anyone. My world was like the light I saw in my office window before passing out, the pain both visual and intellectual.

Joseph said I had not asked the right questions of him. *How do I get rid of you*, I should have asked. He wanted to know if I had guns. Was he afraid I might use them on him? When I described my mini-armory, he said, *You could have taken me out any time you wanted with any of them. Why didn't you?* Was he disappointed that I hadn't? Could I do it? Would I?

I stopped at Hope & Olive for a drink on the way home. Jason Shipley was sitting at the bar, and I slid onto a stool beside him.

"My man," he said, holding his palm up.

I slapped it with my own. "I'm glad to see you."

Jason had taken my introduction to political science course back in the early Seventies. Now in his late fifties, he was one of several psychologists in Franklin County who worked directly with the State Police C-PAC unit, their crime prevention and control branch. A small, wiry man, his thinning hair—once blonde—was almost white. The skin on his face was ruddy from drink and many winters of snowmobiling through the northern forests, his single recreational activity. He wore a long sleeve dress shirt open over a t-shirt bearing a picture of Che Guevara.

"Still fighting the old culture wars," I said, pointing to Che.

He wiggled his fingers. "Not so much fighting as honoring them. Wasn't that a time?"

"Every time is a time," I said.

His eyebrows went up, and he pointed at my eye-patch. "What happened, eye surgery?"

Signaling the bartender, I rested my chin in my hands. "Something like that." I ordered a martini. "On second thought, bring me two," I said.

"You need two drinks so you can jump-start the evening," Jason asked.

"Jace, I don't know what I need. Jan's gotten religion, I've been beaten and terrorized and blinded in one eye, Mimi's being stalked by some smarmy little music teacher at the school where she teaches in North Carolina, and the University wants me to retire. I'm circling the fucking drain."

He rested a hand on my shoulder. "I heard about the beating, and that one of the guys is dead. I didn't know about the rest of it. The local cops brought the Joseph thing to the Staties, and they want me to profile the guy. From what Bourbeau told me it sounds like DID."

"What's that?"

"Dissociative identity disorder."

"And that is what?"

"The soap operas call it multiple personality, *The Three Faces of Eve*, that kind of thing."

"I don't think he's got multiple personalities, just multiple ways of exhibiting the shitty one he's got."

Several martinis later, I finished telling him the story.

He exhaled loudly, and signaled for another drink. "If what you're telling me is right, the guy's crazier than a shithouse rat."

"There's nothing like a clear scientific diagnosis."

He gave me a barstool bow. "Ph.D. courtesy of SUNY-Albany, clarity courtesy of Dr. Jason Shipley."

"So what do I do about him?"

"I'd shoot the fucker if I thought I could get away with it. Short of that, I suggest you call the cops next time you see him."

"Done that. He gets gone fast and comes around unexpectedly. There's no predicting where and when he'll show up."

"He's really got a bunker?"

"In the woods somewhere. It's pretty elaborate."

Jason shook his head. "Scary."

"Thanks."

"I mean it. Scary."

"Want to know what's scarier? He's just part—a big part, but just a part—of what frightens me. My whole life is out of control. Things are falling apart, and the center can't hold much longer."

"I'm sorry, man. I wish I could help, but I'm only a shrink." He raised his beer. "As Dr. Seuss might have said, 'A shrink with a drink.'"

"Maybe I should shoot him."

He looked at me with an expression that could have meant anything.

Tuckerman Court was dark, the street lamps out, the other houses hidden by trees and shrubs already in bloom and leaf. Jan wasn't home when I entered the house, and there were no lights on. I stood in the kitchen, listening to the house: the refrigerator running with a barely perceptible whirr in the compressor, the computer whispering on the corner desk. The aerator in the fish tank gurgled, the cat scratched in her litter box in the back hall, and the quartz clock over the stove clicked second by second. All the background sounds of home, once friendly and comforting, were in that moment disjointed, unsettling, the familiar become alien and menacing.

The phone rang, a loud jangling sound in the dark and strangely unwelcoming house. Ignoring it, I went to a window and looked out over the back yard, bright in the beam of a spotlight mounted on a neighbor's garage. A fox darted across the lawn, drank from the fish pool, and disappeared into the shadow of a hedge. The phone rang until the answering machine picked up and I heard my voice telling the caller to leave a message.

"Hi honey, it's me," Jan said. "Pick up if you're there."

I looked out the window.

"I'm going to be late again," her disembodied voice said. "Another inconsiderate baby." She laughed. "If you get this before it's too late, you could meet me at the hospital and bring a pizza for a midnight snack."

The yard was still, shadows from the lawn furniture stretched over the patio. A bat flitted by, followed by two more. The phone machine clicked off. Reeling from the martinis, I passed on the pizza and the midnight snack.

I woke to sunlight streaming through the bedroom window. Jan was sleeping on her side, facing me, her breathing regular and deep. I hadn't heard her come in and lie down. The clock on the bookcase beside the bed had stopped. Reaching over, I picked my watch up from the bedside table. It was twenty of seven. I slid from under the covers, quietly, so as not to awaken her. Standing at the foot of the bed, I looked at her. In that moment, she was unchanged, the woman I had fallen in love with, had Miriam with, and lived with for nearly forty years. She stirred, mumbled in her sleep, and rolled onto her back, her hair curled around her face.

Were her dreams different now that Jesus had stolen into her heart? To her mind, was I the same person I had been before Jesus, or did her imagining of him alter her imagining of me? Did it change her imagining of Miriam? It seemed to have transformed her, although beyond her words and an eerie quietude that seemed semi-comatose to me, I had no way of knowing how. And where had Jesus come from? In what ways was he related to the Jesus of scripture, to the Jesus of history, to the Jesus of the many and various denominations, churches, sects, priests, preachers, and madmen that have tried to interpret him through the ages and represent those interpretations in the world? Was he a concept she unknowingly created, or the result of some transcendent moment she believed she had experienced? Either one she might have identified as Jesus, because doing so would be the easiest and most socially acceptable way of explaining her feelings about the experience.

There may have been a Jesus who influenced disaffected people in Roman Jerusalem and its environs. There is historical evidence suggesting he did live, although a long-standing classified ad in *The Nation* promises proof he never existed, that Christianity is based on a hoax. I believe the two positions are not mutually exclusive. I don't need to deny Jesus' existence in order to regard the religions built on faith in him to be hoaxes.

I was furious at Jesus. Whatever he meant to Jan, he was taking my wife from me. Men have killed other men for that.

After dressing, I went downstairs, brought in the morning paper, made a pot of coffee, and watched the newsmouths on CNN explain the subtleties of the primary election in West Virginia, citing political scientists as they made predictions about the remaining primaries and what they meant to the candidates, in spite of what the candidates said they meant. I switched to MSNBC. Other newsmouths were saying the same things.

"Hi Babe," Jan said coming into the kitchen wearing a sleek silk dressing gown, looking better than I'd seen her in weeks. Leaning over, she gave me a kiss and ran her fingers through my hair. "What's up in the world?"

I rattled the paper and made a face. "According to this morning's *Recorder*, the town's school finances are in the tank again, and ants in Texas they think crawled out of a shipping container from Asia have spread over five counties and are shorting out electronics and eating the eggs of a species of endangered quail. Things are worse in Iraq, better in Afghanistan, or worse in Afghanistan and better in Iraq. It doesn't matter, they're terrible in Sudan. Earthquakes and cyclones have devastated China and Myanmar, which, as you know, was once Burma and might become Burma again, and dams in China might collapse and Burma might get hit by another cyclone. Other than that, there's no news except the dog died."

"You make it sound like the world's in chaos."

"It isn't? On top of all that crap, you're being sued for malpractice, I'm being stalked by a total whack job who blinded me and is now my new best friend, and Mimi's being followed around by another whack job who stands outside her apartment and croons her name all night long. If that doesn't amount to a fucked-up, chaotic cosmos, I hate to think what does."

Without replying, Jan poured herself a cup of coffee. Toasting and buttering a couple of English muffins, she gave me one and took the other along with her coffee out the kitchen door and sat on the back patio. Sunlight glistened in her hair. I turned the TV off and joined her with the second muffin and my coffee, squatting on a blue foam pool mat we kept there for sunbathing.

We sat without talking. A cardinal sang from the pine grove behind the house, and two chipmunks were nosing around the fish pond where I had seen the fox. The neighborhood was waking up, but for the moment it was peaceful. Soon the sounds of lawnmowers and hedge clippers would drown out the cardinal's song, and children's voices calling from yard to yard, dogs barking, cars and delivery trucks on the street would dominate the day.

"I love you." Jan looked at me over the rim of her coffee mug.

"Me too," I said.

"Me too what?"

"Me too, I love you."

"How much?" It was an old game, and it felt good to be playing it again. She hadn't been playful in a long time, and I'd been no better.

"Ten," I said.

She pouted. "Is that all?"

"On a scale of minus twenty to plus three," I said.

She was about to continue when we heard the clacking of hooves from the street, and the sudden chatter of excited voices. We rushed to the front yard just as a moose walked down the middle of Tuckerman Court, followed by our neighbors, their cameras clicking, their voices cheerful and animated.

"Amazing," Mrs. Minsky said, as she crossed the street to stand beside me. "It's obviously coming from the park."

"But where's it going," Jan said. "There's nothing but houses and downtown in the direction it's headed."

"It could go left up Highland and back into the park," Mrs. Minsky said. The moose turned right, toward downtown. "Well, look at that beast. You just never know what's going to happen next with these critters. Did you hear about the Andrews over on Mountain Road?"

"What," I asked. Mountain Road was just over the hill, a quarter of a mile away.

She took a deep breath and shook her head. "Bears. They had a couple of bears in their yard, a mother and her cub. Darn things tore down her bird feeders and something, probably those damned bears, ate most of her cat. There wasn't much left but some fur and part of the skull." She tugged at my shirtsleeve. "How're you doing, Tom?"

Jan put her hand to her mouth before I could answer. "How terrible."

"It left a big pile of dung, too. Imagine, the damned bear eats her cat and shits it right back out in her yard."

Jan suppressed a laugh. "I doubt if the transition from cat to excretion happened that quickly."

"It's disgusting, whether or not the cat was in the dung. I guess that's what happens when the wilderness comes into town."

"The wilderness is everywhere," Jan said.

"There was a bear in the parking lot over at the community college last fall," Chip LaSalle from up the street said.

Mrs. Minsky shrugged. "Greenfield might as well be in the jungle." She turned to me. "So, how are you doing, Tom?"

"Fine," I said.

She gave me a look that said she recognized my voice was too perky, but she would leave the subject of my recovery alone. "They never caught those men, did they?"

"One of them's dead. The other one's still running around the area."

"Animals," she said, her face twisted in contempt. "They find the other one, they should take him out behind the jailhouse and shoot him in the back of the head. I don't believe in capital punishment, mind you, but some people don't deserve to live. It'd save us all a lot of grief if you could just shoot them."

"That was my first moose," I said to Jan, as we walked back to the patio.

"Mine too, outside of the zoo."

I sat on an Adirondack chair. After a moment's hesitation, she sat on the arm and leaned against my shoulder. "I don't have any appointments this morning."

"How did that happen?"

"I told Jennifer to keep the morning open. I don't have to go in until after one. And you don't have any classes."

"And?"

"We could do things."

"Things?"

She fiddled with my ear. "You know, things." She moved to the pool float and lay down, opening her dressing gown.

"Things sounds like a fine idea." I joined her on the mat. She was dry, and I was half flaccid, but we touched each other, and the time passed tenderly and sweetly.

After an indeterminate time, she laughed and kissed my shoulder. "It certainly isn't like it was thirty years ago."

"Or five, even," I said.

"I love you, Tommy."

"All these years," I said.

She nodded in silence. I watched her lying there, her robe still open, the sun soft on her skin and hair. Her breasts were brown, each leg, each arm. Looking back at me, she laughed.

"Did you see that chipmunk on the rock beside the pond?"

"I saw one earlier."

"This was just now. I was looking over your shoulder, and he was staring at me." A hummingbird flew by, small cyclones from its wings rippling the down on her shoulder.

I smiled, and rising up, resting on my elbow, I touched her brown skin with wildness in my heart.

After showers and a change of clothing, we ate cucumber sandwiches on the front porch, washing them down with ice water, and we still had time to relax before Jan's first appointment. Tuckerman Court was quiet. The red-tails were back riding the thermals, and the neighbor's cat joined us. Curling up beside Jan on the couch, it rested its head against her leg and began to purr. Her hand fell to its back, and she slowly petted it.

"This has been nice," she said. "I've been pretending that everything is peaceful and safe, and it almost worked."

"What happened?"

"The Whipple's cat, Tildy Mathews, and thinking of them led to me thinking about Miriam, and then about you and that Joseph person."

"What do Tildy Mathews and the cat have to do with all that?"

"One of the last things we talked about was her cat. She was wondering if there was any truth to the old superstition that cats will suck a baby's breath away." Her laugh was rueful. "Isn't it amazing, that in this day and age someone would ask such a question? She was a very sweet and innocent woman. They were both sweet and innocent, Tildy and her husband, Charlie. And so young, Tommy, so very young."

"And now he's coming after you."

"I understand. He's broken-hearted, and needs someone to blame for losing his wife and baby."

"It's not fair," I said.

"I can take it. I've got insurance, and I know I did the best I could. I do worry about you and Mimi." Her voice remained even, composed, and her expression was relaxed.

"How can you be so calm?"

She smiled and tilted her head. "Jesus."

"I'd almost forgotten," I said.

"I haven't. He's with me every moment."

I couldn't resist. "Even naked on the patio with me?"

Her smile didn't waver. "Always."

"A three-way, eh?"

She laughed. "I suppose you could look at it that way."

I stood and walked to the edge of the porch, looking out at the street, to the spot where Joseph and Randy had knocked me down and begun kicking me. "Everything seemed so normal this morning."

"Seemed normal? Babe, it was normal."

"With you and Jesus and me rubbing together?"

"He knows what people who love each other do."

"Do you think he did it, with Mary Magdalene, or anybody else?"

Picking up the cat and nuzzling it against her neck, she rose and stood beside me, leaning her knees against the railing. "I'd like to think so. People who deny sex and blame religion for it are sad, and some of them do some very sick things, like that priest in Shelburne."

"Father LaSalle," I said. Guy LaSalle, a priest in Shelburne, was among the first to be named, indicted, and defrocked in the priest sexual scandals that rocked the church in Massachusetts and across the country. A serial abuser of young boys, it was also revealed at the time of his trial that he was the only suspect in the murder of an altar boy in Brattleboro more than twenty years before. There had never been sufficient evidence to try him, but the boy's parents and the chief investigator were convinced of his guilt.

"Jesus doesn't want people to destroy others and themselves and blame it on him."

"I don't get this Jesus thing." I sighed and leaned against the railing.

Her response was sharp and quick. "I told you, it isn't a thing."

"I know, Jesus entered your heart and told you to follow him the rest of your days."

She slipped her free arm around my waist. "Has that harmed you?"

"Not yet." I hoped she didn't hear the resentment and reservation in my tone.

"And we've had a wonderful morning together?"

"I have."

"Me too," she whispered.

We stood there, not talking, for a long time. She kept her arm around my waist, and I rested my hand on top of her wrist. The cat purred. No cars drove up or down Tuckerman Court. No neighbors walked their dogs. No lawnmowers, leaf-blowers, no noise beyond the ambient sounds of the town, sirens in the distance, traffic on nearby streets, airplanes circling for landings in Turners Falls, the rumble of railroad cars across the river in the East Deerfield switching yards.

If moments could be encapsulated and kept in a chest for viewing later in life, this was one I would keep and treasure against those moments of age, pain, and loss, of incapacity and loneliness I know lie in the years ahead. I filed the memory, knowing it would have to be enough.

"Store up good memories like squirrels store nuts," my grandfather had told me when I was eleven. He had taken me hiking on the High Ledges, and we stood beside a blueberry thicket near the overlook.

He was in his eighties then. My grandmother suffered from dementia, probably Alzheimer's, her mind wandering, her thoughts and moods subject to random shifts that seemed to bear no relationship to what was going on around her. She was in a nursing home, and Gramp was living with my aunt and uncle. In my childish way, I understood he was storing up that moment for himself. We were picking blueberries, eating more than we put in the paper bags we had carried up there with us. He had put his bag down and knelt on one knee beside me, the August sun on the side of his face, his white hair tousled by the breeze. He took my hand. "Old age is like winter; you'll need to dig up the memories you've saved and chew them over."

"I've got to go," Jan said. Removing her arm, she stepped away and set the cat down on the steps leading to the sidewalk. "I love you, Tommy," she said, and walked into the house, returning at once with her pocketbook, her car keys jingling in her hand.

The phone rang.

"Let's meet for lunch," Joseph said as soon as I picked up.

"Why?"

I could hear his smile over the line. "Because that's what friends do. They meet for lunch, have a drink after work, go fishing together, have dinner with their wives and girl friends tagging along."

"We're not friends," I said.

"I am your friend, Thomas." His tone was not friendly. "We will have lunch together. I suggest The Wagon Wheel on Route 2 in Gill. It's close, and it's got good food."

"It's late for lunch, and I'm not hungry. I already had lunch with Jan."

"Meet me there in half an hour, and bring your cell phone." He hung up.

I called Bourbeau, telling him about Joseph's call. "If you came, you could nail the son-of-a-bitch."

"Sorry, it's out of town. You'll have to call the Gill police or the Staties. I'd go with the Staties, if I was you."

"How about you calling them and explaining the situation."

He ignored me. "Call Ed Schilling at the Shelburne barracks. Him and me hang out together. We've talked about your case a lot."

"What's his take on it?"

"Not much, since it's a local case, except they got that C-PAC shrink thinking about it, for all the good he'll do, but Ed just shakes his head and says that Greenfield is one major fucked-up town, which no doubt it is, what with the Walker brothers last year and all the whack jobs we've got roaming up and down Main Street pan-handling."

He was right about the Walker brothers. Abetted by their mother, Shirley, three of them—Percy, Archie, and Elmore—along with two cousins—Wilfred and Arthur Gagnon—had imprisoned a local street kid named Fluffy Parker in their house. They handcuffed him naked to a radiator on the second floor, starved him, beat him, raped him, shocked him with bare wires on his testicles, made him eat feces, and urinated on him, along with a number of other things the papers said were too vile to print.

Fluffy Parker, like the Walker brothers, was an outsider, one of those people whose existence does not intrude on our own. We see them on the street corners, leaning against the walls in front of temporary employment offices promising same day pay for work, the young girls and women who bear their children hanging around with them, littering the pavements with cigarette butts and spittle, their own children in stained, torn strollers passed one from one to another, stolen, or bought at the Salvation Army store.

As a girl, Miriam saw the Walkers and Gagnons at school. When *The Recorder* broke the story about Fluffy's captivity, abuse, and death, she told us tales of the Walkers during their shared school years. Smoking dope and drinking alcohol, even in their single digit years, they and their friends terrorized the playground and disrupted school rooms. Elmore, she told us one night at dinner, often smelled of shit and piss, and by the age of ten had already lost his teeth.

After the Parker kid died, the Walkers and Gagnons buried his body in the Montague Plains, a high flat and sandy area a few miles across the river from Greenfield. A couple of dogs dug it up, and one of their owners got curious about the bones it was gnawing on the front porch. In the course of their investigation, the police discovered that many of the Walkers' friends and neighbors had stopped by to watch Percy beat Fluffy. He'd show him off as if he were a new pet, give people a paddle of one-inch lumber, and ask them to hit him.

"Stuff a sock in his mouth first," he was reported as telling one woman who admitted to the police she had broken Fluffy's wrist with the paddle.

The three Walkers and the Gagnons were convicted of various degrees of murder and manslaughter. Percy, the ringleader, along with Archie and Elmore, got life in Cedar Junction. The Gagnons were sent away for twenty years, and Shirley got a suspended sentence. Two younger brothers weren't indicted. No one would testify that either of them had ever been in the

Deerfield Street house where Fluffy had been tortured and killed. Like their brothers and cousins, they were known stoners, but on the Fluffy count, they were legally clean. The friends and neighbors who joined in on the fun got off by bearing witness against the Walkers and Gagnons.

"You're not going to help me," I said to Bourbeau.

"I can't. It's out of my jurisdiction, and besides, like I keep telling you, we haven't got the money to pay me to go out of town."

"So what do I do?"

He sighed. "All right, I'll call Schilling for you and give him a heads up, but you've got to call him yourself to make arrangements for him to meet you in Gill."

I called the State Police. Ed Schilling was off duty, making extra money standing by while a road crew worked on I-91bridge repairs. I asked to speak to someone in charge, but after waiting on hold for five minutes, I was disconnected. I called the Gill police and explained the situation. They promised to stop by the Wagon Wheel at the time I was to meet Joseph. If there was a warrant out for him, the chief assured me, they would arrest him.

"I don't know if there's a warrant," I said. "If there is, it's probably for a John Doe. I don't know if Joseph is his real name, and I've got no idea what his full name might be. He just goes by Joseph."

"You don't know much, do you," the chief said.

"Just that this guy scares the shit out of me."

"All I can promise is that somebody'll stop by and take a look, Mr. Rabberman."

"Rutherford." A chill ran though me. I had lived my adult life as an insider. On the outside as a child, I did well in school, in spite of the poverty I was raised in, and got a scholarship to Amherst, and scholarships and good financial aid for graduate school. Since then, I've had medical insurance, and I've lived in nice homes in good neighborhoods, all as a result of my employment at a state university and my wife's income from her medical practice. A level of prestige accompanies my life as a university professor, and as the husband of a successful and well regarded physician. Added to those comforts, to ease my old age I had a pension from the state, and Jan's investments promised additional old age support.

Now I had been shunted outside by a system short-changed both literally and metaphorically. The national obsession with terrorism, and the corrupt people in control of our national government who exploited it, had resulted in monies and will being diverted into false wars and wasteful exercises, resulting in huge profits for the hangers-on of politicians in positions of making decisions on those matters. Little was left for local domestic needs. The terrors that face individuals in their towns, their neighborhoods, and their homes were of no consequence to those decision makers, and we were increasingly left on our own to deal with under-funded schools, libraries, fire, police, and public works departments: all those services of our home towns and cities that contribute to the civilized nature of our lives.

The Walkers and those with like shortages of resources—mental, financial and social—were the outsiders. Knowing that did not warm the chill. Suddenly, I was on the outside again. Not like the Walkers, but still on the outside, looking in at a system I had come to think of as being there to protect those of us who believed we were insiders. Now that system lacked the resources, will, and integration to help me. The bubble of comfort has thin walls, easily penetrated. Only the way the light hits it gives those walls the illusion of protectiveness.

As if to belie my paranoia, the Gill cruiser sat in the parking lot at the Wagon Wheel. Mack Bandowski, a former student in my Constitutional Law class, stood beside it, waving as I pulled in.

"Hey, Professor Rutherford," he said, waddling toward me, his hand extended. We shook, and he looked around. "What's this guy look like?"

"Hard to say. He's into changing his identity. One day he'll look and talk like a Mafia punk, the next he's like something out of *The Treasure of the Sierra Madre*."

"Badges badges, we don't need no stinkin' badges," he laughed. "I can't stay long. I'm the only one on duty today, and there's a budget meeting at Town Hall. I might have to go part-time next year, and I've got to talk to the muckety-mucks about what that'll mean for the town. You see your guy anywhere?"

I looked around and shook my head.

"Well anyway, I'll stick around for a few more minutes, but I can't stay long."

I was about to thank him when my cell phone rang. Taking a few steps away from Mack, I answered.

"You shouldn't have brought the cops," Joseph said. "Don't you trust me?"

"No." I waved at Mack and pointed to my cell mouthing, "He's on the phone."

"Where," he said.

I shrugged my shoulders. "They know you're here," I said into the mouthpiece.

"Ah, but I'm not. It's just that I understand you. I knew you'd call them, and you just confirmed it. You shouldn't've done that, Thomas. It was a very bad mistake. Now I'm angry with you."

"You weren't angry when you and Randy beat and kicked and blinded me?"

"I was angry, but not specifically at you, just at what you represented to me at that moment. Now it's specific. You've betrayed our friendship, Thomas. That makes me sad and mad and leaves me wondering how I should respond, what steps I must take to prove the strength of my friendship, to show you how much I care for you."

"You could leave me alone."

He chuckled. "Right, and that would deprive me of your company."

"And I of yours, which would be a boon."

"Don't worry, old chap," he said, falling into a British accent. "I'll think of something appropriate. You must, however, understand that whatever happens will be entirely on your head. Had you not put me to this test, I wouldn't have to take any action to prove myself to you, would I?"

"You've proved more than enough," I said, but the line was dead.

Nine

Five days passed quietly. No surprise visits from Joseph. No phone calls. No further suggestions from R.C. Alexander that I take an early retirement. Jan and I had quiet breakfasts each morning, watched television, read or watched rented movies in the evenings, and went to bed, once in each other's arms. Our lovemaking was slow and careful, lacking the heat of passion that once drove us. I managed a single erection, and she was dry. She used to laughingly refer to me, in private of course, by the nickname, "Tommy Hard-on," so predictable was my response, even to the *word* sex. Now we are never sure when I will rise to the occasion, or if she welcome me with all-natural lubrication.

There was little conversation during our daily lives beyond communicating over necessities, but the time was peaceful, and the lack of discussion seemed natural rather than awkward, at least to me. Jan said no more about Jesus, and I didn't ask about him.

The weather was surprisingly cool for late May. April had been its cruel self, teasing New England with nearly two weeks of warm days and almost southern summery nights, but in late May, I had kept the woodstove burning for six nights, and wore sweaters covered by a light jacket when I took my daily walk. There were reports of light snow in northern Vermont and the adjacent Adirondacks.

"Where's global warming when you really want it," people would joke when the topic of the cold spring weather came up.

My brother, Barry, called from Elkhart, Indiana, where he practiced in a small law firm dedicated to environmental causes. We talked about politics and pollution and the recent Presidential primary in his state.

"People are so fucked up," he said. "When I went in to vote, I passed a group of Obama supporters, holding signs and greeting people as they walked into the polls. Going in, I met a woman I know, Glenda Allen, a lawyer in another firm. She's attractive, intelligent and, I always thought, pretty progressive. She's active in the local Democratic party, on several boards of forward-looking organizations, all that, and still, she pointed back at the Obama people and asked 'how could anybody vote for that Buckwheat?' Where's her sense of things? I wouldn't be surprised if she ends up voting for McCain rather than for a man of mixed heritage who represents her best interests. Jesus, Tommy, what's this country coming to? Don't people have any sense?"

"Don't get me started," I said, and shifted the conversation to family.

We spent the next ten minutes talking about our children, the states of our marriages, our aches, pains, and medications. When I was in the hospital, Jan had called and told him about the beating, but he knew nothing of Joseph stalking me afterwards. I filled him in.

"Shoot the fucker," he said.

"I'll need a good lawyer. You applying for the job?"

"I'm out of state, and I don't defend criminals."

"Would it be criminal to shoot someone who's done all these things to me?"

He chuckled. "Might be criminal not to shoot him."

We chatted for a few more minutes, our conversation ending with my promise that Jan and I would visit him and his wife Vicky in August, when boating on Lake Erie would be at its prime.

Late on Friday, the fifth night of the cold snap, Jan went to bed early. I worked late in my study, laboring over an article on willful ignorance and voter irrationality which the editor of *Theoretical Politics Quarterly* had asked me to write for the fall issue. It was a bleak task, made bleaker by Barry's description of Glenda Allen. I worked in fits and starts, periodically spurred on by listening to the prattlings of newsmouths on CNN, their hourly manufactured analyses of the Presidential primaries bearing witness to my theories.

I took frequent breaks, going from the study to the living room to the kitchen, looking for something to nosh on, stepping outside for fresh air, and then back in to rummage through the refrigerator and the munchies cabinet. Soon I tired of moving aimlessly in and out of the house, and decided to find relief by dipping into the most recent account of life in

Botswana's *No. 1 Ladies' Detective Agency.*

I read little fiction. It seduces us from confronting reality. In my republic, as in Plato's, there will be no place for the sweet distractions of art, at least until people are willing to face up to the truths of our existence and deal with them in a fully informed and analytical fashion, which will never happen. Since I do not live in my republic, and never will, I opened the book. Raising it to my nose, I breathed in the combined odors of paper, ink, binding, and glue. It was a comforting smell, and I ran my fingers over the smooth surface of the pages, then riffed through them, watching the changing patterns of letters, sentences, and paragraphs as the pages moved quickly by.

Removing the dust jacket, I set it in a magazine rack and stretched out on the couch to read. I fell asleep while driving with Mma Ramotswe in her ancient and tiny white van through the Botswana countryside outside Gaborone. I sat up, wide awake and jangling, as the front door slammed open and Miriam came into the room calling for me.

"Daddy," she shrieked, and ran to the couch, nearly knocking me over. "He's dead, Daddy. Somebody killed him. I was out a concert with friends, and when they dropped me off at home, I found Johnny Shook's body propped against the door to my apartment. I freaked. I just ran out, got in the car and started driving. I drove all night, Daddy. It was so horrible, I couldn't stay."

She was shaking, crying, and breathing irregularly in deep gasps. "Somebody slit his throat, and his head was lolling off to the side like it was going to fall onto the floor. There was blood all over, even running under the door into my apartment, and they'd put a ribbon on his forehead, you know, that fancy sticky backed kind people put on Christmas presents they wrap up and don't want to bother tying a ribbon on, and there was a note stuck to his chest with a pin."

"What kind of note?" My heart was pounding.

She reached into her pocket and pulled out a crumpled piece of paper. "Here, I grabbed it before I ran. I don't know why."

Taking it, I read, *Dear Mimi, hope you like your present.*

"Mimi, not Miriam?"

"That's one of the freakiest things about it. Nobody down there calls me

Mimi. I'm Miriam. I don't think they even know I've got a nickname."

"Was anything else there?"

"Just the note. I took it and ran down the stairs, got in my car, and started driving. I didn't even know I was coming home until I hit the Virginia line."

She was disheveled, her hair going in every direction, her face pale, eyes wide and wild, her clothes rumpled, and her blouse spotted with brown stains, probably from juggling cardboard containers of coffee as she drove.

"You called the police?"

Shaking her head, still breathing in hard, wrenching gasps, she said, "I just ran. I was so frightened. I still am."

I pulled her close, one arm around her shoulder, the other cradling her head. "It's okay now. You're safe. But we'll have to deal with the police down there."

"Not tonight."

I touched her hair and ran my hand down her cheek. "Not tonight."

I studied her face: my daughter, her nose and chin so like my own, her mouth and eyes like her mother's. The eyes stopped me. They were red-rimmed with black circles beneath them. I imagined her driving the Interstates through the night, rubbing those eyes with the back of her hand, hours of bucking the heavy truck traffic on I-81 up through the Shenandoah into the Pennsylvania countryside and across 84 to 91, panicky and over-tired, the sounds of the car and the clicking of her turn signals as she shifted lanes amplified by weariness and the late, dark hours.

"Why would anyone do that, Daddy. Kill him, I mean, and leave him leaning against my door?"

I shook my head, keeping silent.

"He was annoying, but sad, too, and harmless." She gave me a wan smile mixed with a trace of nervous laughter. "Singing my name under my window, once even on a rainy night, standing there drenched and shivering."

"You've got to admit, it's a little creepy."

She sniffed. "More than creepy. I wanted it to stop, but I didn't want him dead, just chilled out enough to know he shouldn't be carrying on like that. Why would somebody kill him, Daddy?"

"Maybe he was selling drugs, or using them and he owed somebody money."

"Not Johnny. He was straight, except for his obsession with me. Besides, if it was over drugs, why did they prop him against my door, and why that note?"

"I don't know, honey," I said. But I did. *Understand that whatever happens will be entirely on your head.* "There's no accounting for what some people do." *Had you not put me to this test I wouldn't have to take any action to prove myself to you.*

"Where's Mom," she asked.

"In bed. Go wake her up."

"I'll wait until morning. I couldn't go through explaining it again tonight."

"Want me to tell her?"

"No. I'll be up to it tomorrow. Right now I need sleep. I just want to crawl into my old bed and try pretending I'd never left here."

"Things'll look better in the morning," I said, voicing a parent's meaningless and untrue attempt at reassurance.

"No, Daddy, they won't. I just won't be so tired, and there'll be a few more hours between me and the time I found Johnny's body."

She went upstairs, and I lay back down on the couch. Despite the disruption of her arrival and the news she brought, I was half asleep ten minutes later when I heard the sound of the refrigerator door closing in the kitchen. Thinking Jan or Miriam had crept downstairs for a snack, I got up and went in.

"Howdy, pardner." Joseph stood in the middle of the room, a glass of milk in his hand. Wearing a Stetson hat, a western shirt with mother of pearl buttons, tight jeans, and what looked to be alligator boots. He had two silver six shooters holstered on a black leather gun belt slung around his hips. His hair hung out from under the hat, falling over his forehead, Gary Cooper style. On his upper lip was a thick handlebar mustache. A tin star was pinned over his heart, the word "Sheriff" embossed on it. He raised the glass.

"Here's milk in your eye, pard," he said, and drank it down.

"You son-of-a-bitch," I said, moving toward him.

Putting the glass down, he rested his right hand on the butt of a pistol, and raised his left hand to his face, waving his forefinger back and forth.

"I just might be the meanest son-of-a-bitch in the world," he said. "Then again, I might not be. I don't rightly know, there's so many sons-of-bitches. Or is it son-of-a-bitches. Sumbitches, maybe is what I should say. And I don't rightly know if I am mean. Being mean is something I wouldn't want to be called, even by myself, so I wouldn't be inclined to file memories of meanness away in my brain."

"You're a mean sumbitch," I said.

He shrugged.

"How'd you get in here?"

He reached in his breast pocket and pulled out a key. "I reckon with this."

I grabbed it from him.

"I got another, boy. I got ways of getting in anywhere I want to get in: people, keys, all kinds of ways."

"You killed that music teacher and left his body at Miriam's door."

He shook his head. "Never been to North Carolina, pard. Been to Texas, though. Ever been to Texas?"

"What do you want? And don't wake up my wife and daughter."

"Incredible place, Texas," he spoke in a near whisper. "I went to the Alamo where all them heroes died, Davy Crockett and them others, Bill Travis, Jim Bowie, although they say Bowie was sick in his cot and that they killed him in bed, and Billy Bob Thornton, all killed by Santa Anna and his men."

"Billy Bob Thornton wasn't at the Alamo," I said, before realizing he'd once again tricked me into participating in a conversation with him.

"The hell you say. I seen him there. It was in a moving picture, and they killed him dead right there at the Alamo, the Mexicans did. That's why that Lou Dobbs fella on CNN wants all them illegal Mexicans kicked out of the country, in retribution for them killing Billy Bob."

"Billy Bob Thornton is an actor and movie director," I said.

"Exactly. A good one, too. That's why Lou Dobbs is so pissed off. Them Mexicans is sneaking across the border, taking jobs from hard-working

Americans, and killing people like Billy Bob Thornton. Lou Dobbs is going to put a stop to all that."

"Do you really believe that?"

"I do right now." He picked at his teeth with a fingernail. "Who knows what I'll believe tomorrow. Sometimes I forget all about Lou Dobbs. Other times, I think he's a lunatic. Today he speaks for who I am. I ain't always the same me, you know."

"You're fucking crazy," I said, softly enough not to carry upstairs and wake Jan and Miriam, if she was lucky enough to get to sleep.

"That's getting to be a right boring line, Thomas, and there's no call to add vulgarities to it. If a man can't express hisself without resorting to profanity and vulgarity, he ain't got much of a mind, and he ain't going to win any friends."

Weary, I collapsed onto a stool. His use of the word boring struck me, and I realized I was bored by his ever shifting personas and his affectation of morality bolstered by his claim of forgetfulness. Under normal circumstances, I would have been frightened, but I found myself disinterested in him and his nonsensical rants and theories. My response to what I once might have found frightening was weakening. I felt that my psychological immune system was kicking in.

"Who killed Johnny Shook?"

"That the music teacher you was accusing me of killing?"

"You know it is."

His nod was barely perceptible.

"Never laid eyes on him."

"But you gave orders."

"I ain't that powerful, pard. It strikes me that a man who wants to give orders to have another man killed has got to either have something awful potent over them he wants to do the killing, or be a good friend to them and have a compelling reason to want them to do the killing. Besides, I would think giving orders to kill a man would be something no one would want to remember. I certainly wouldn't like to carry that kind of a memory around with me."

"You are fucking, fucking crazy."

He smiled. "Vulgarity again, boy, but you're half right. I do go just a tad crazy when things don't go as I expect them to go. Like any man, I suppose, and that should make you think twice about crossing me, about betraying my friendship like you did over there in Gill that day you was talking to the policeman." He said PO-liceman. "Now I've had my milk, and we've had our chat. You just trundle along to bed, and I'll mosey on out and lock up after myself."

"Go. I'll lock up."

"Help yourself."

He put down the empty glass and let himself out the door, leaning back in before shutting it. "Reckon that little girl of yours is gonna sleep better tonight. I hope something comes along to ease your wife's problems."

I didn't call the police. No point. Joseph was my problem, and Barry had supplied the answer. I brought a step ladder up from the basement and set it up in the middle of the kitchen floor. With a flashlight in hand, I climbed up, lifted a panel of the drop ceiling, and reached around until I found the blanket I had wrapped around the guns I'd stored there years before. I pulled it out, sneezing as dust and mouse droppings fell through the air. Laying the blanket on the floor, I unwrapped it. The Smith and Wesson .22, its black .38 Police Special frame still glistening, lay beside the 1937 Marlin .22, and Winchester 12 gauge.

Rewrapping the rifle and shotgun in the blanket, I put them back above the ceiling, cleaned up the mess, and put the ladder away. I oiled the pistol, regretting that it took only .22 bullets. A full .38 would be more effective. I went to my study, opened the safe, and found the box of .22 hollow points I had locked in there at the same time I had hidden the guns in the kitchen.

Taking one out, I held it between my thumb and forefinger, the brass casing reflecting the light. A small indenture in the lead missile was the only sop to my regret. The value of the hollow point lies in the way it opens up when it hits. A round point bullet will easily pass through a target, endangering other people who may be in the area, often leaving the person you are determined to stop still coming at you. A hollow point flowers, causing maximum damage with a far greater chance of stopping whoever is threatening you.

With a bullet as small as a .22, I wanted as much stopping power as possible. I took the box to the kitchen, spread a dish towel on the table, and emptied the bullets onto it. Using a heavy knife, I widened the holes in the tip of each bullet, increasing their ability to flower once they entered Joseph's chest. Finished, I chambered six bullets in the pistol, put the rest in my briefcase, and cleaned up the mess. I didn't want Jan or Mimi to find any traces of my work when they came downstairs in the morning.

Holding the pistol in both hands and squinting as I aimed it at a midpoint in the room, I squeezed off three imaginary rounds, accompanying them with the same plosive vocal sounds I used to make when I was a kid playing cowboys and outlaws. I am comfortable with guns. I began shooting at the age of six, when my mother's uncle would take me off for two weeks camping in the White Mountains where he taught me to fish, swim, and canoe. Each day, we would spend hours plinking away with his twenty-two rifle. I was proud of the well-clustered holes in my paper targets. I had not shot a gun in many years, until last summer, when a friend with an arsenal hidden in the toolbox of his Ford F-250 took me shooting at a gun club in Williamsburg, just west of Northampton. I hoped my one eye was still true.

It was four in the morning when I finished. After hiding the pistol and ammunition in my briefcase, I went out on the porch, lay down on the wicker couch, and covered myself with a down comforter we keep there. I fell asleep imagining Joseph's face as the hollow point .22 flowered in his chest, blood flowing red over his heart. Who could fault me?

Saturday morning, Mimi told her story as Jan buried her face in her hands. A night's sleep had calmed her. She spoke softly, without the shaking and sobbing that had accompanied the version I first heard.

"Was it Joseph," Jan asked, when Mimi finished.

"At least indirectly," I said. "He once said he had a friend down there, although he claimed to be unable to remember his name."

"Miriam has to call the Boone police," she said.

Miriam touched her mother's hand. "I have to go back down, Mom. After all, I do live there, and I plan to stay. I have to go straighten this all out."

"Not alone," said Jan. "I'll go with you. I can get someone to cover for me."

Miriam didn't argue.

I didn't offer to go. I had other things to do, and having both of them gone would make doing them easier.

While Miriam called the Boone police and explained why she had fled, Jan began to pack. I followed her upstairs.

"What brought all this misery into our lives, Tommy?"

"Jesus."

She took a sharp insuck of breath and turned to me, glaring. "Jesus is love. This is not love. It's fearful, it's hate, it's everything that Jesus stands against."

I looked into her eyes and spoke as softly as I could. "In a way it was Jesus. It all began after you told me you had let him into your heart."

"One doesn't let Jesus into one's heart. When Jesus decides to enter, he enters. One must accept that he has entered."

"And if one doesn't accept it?"

"Jesus will just keep filling your heart until you're so full and ready to burst wide open that you have to accept him."

"And if you still don't?"

"I reckon you just burst."

"Sounds like rape to me."

She whirled. "You won't understand until he comes to you."

"That was a stupid thing for me to say." I opened my arms in concession to her position. "When you told me Jesus had entered your heart, I was at a loss. After we'd talked for a few minutes, I was so bummed and confused that I wandered outside, not knowing what to think, not knowing what to do. If I hadn't been out there at that moment, Joseph and Randy would have walked on by, would have never come up Tuckerman Court, and none of this would have happened."

"They would have found someone else to beat up."

"Maybe, maybe not. If I hadn't been standing on the street, they probably would have kept on up Highland Avenue into the park. Walking there in the early spring might have changed their mindset. Who knows how they might have reacted to the soft greens of early sprouts and buds on the trees, the rush of water in the streams, and the sun coming through the still-bare branches."

"That's an absurd, utterly unacceptable position, Tommy. Jesus is not to blame."

"Jesus is responsible for great evil. Look at the preachers who blame the destruction from the 9/11 terrorists and hurricane Katrina on Jesus, claiming he's punishing people for what they say are depraved lifestyles."

"That's not Jesus. That's sick men using his name to justify their own perversions."

"It's an old argument," I said. "We're not going to resolve it here. All I said was that if you hadn't picked that moment to tell me about you and Jesus, I wouldn't have been so upset that I went outside and met up with Joseph and Randy. If I hadn't met up with them, none of these horrible events would have taken place. I'd still be seeing in three dimensions. Johnny Shook would still be alive and driving our daughter to distraction. Joseph wouldn't be turning up in my life on a regular basis."

I didn't add that I wouldn't be on the verge of becoming a murderer.

"So it's my fault for telling you about Jesus."

"No. It's the result of a confluence of events, random and unpredictable. Neither of us should feel guilty. It happened. It wouldn't have happened if you'd told me about Jesus entering your heart the day before or the day after, or even at dinner that same day. But that random and unpredictable confluence of events has led us to this moment, and to whatever will come after it, which will, in all probability, be another confluence of random and unpredictable events."

She sat on the edge of the bed. "You believe life is without order or meaning?"

"The only order and meaning is that we create to make our lives work as we attempt to pursue happiness."

"You're wrong. There is meaning to life, even if we can't grasp it with our limited human minds. That's why Jesus is willing to come into our hearts, to help us see beyond what appears to us as chaos, if we will only let him."

Sitting beside her, I took her hand. The veins on its back were bluer and more pronounced than when I had first held them, the skin rough and marked by brown spots. Raising it to my lips, I kissed her fingers. They were skilled fingers, practiced at helping children enter the world with the least amount of harm to them and to their mothers. Fingers adept at cutting into a human body, repairing its damage, and closing it back up. Perhaps her concept of Jesus was a metaphor for her own need to enter into someone and save them.

"I don't understand anything," I said. "I have no depth of vision."

"None of this is my fault," she said.

"No," I said. "It isn't"

After Jan and Miriam left, I paced from room to room. It was late Saturday, and I had no idea when Joseph would again contact me or appear. I only knew he would. After all, I was his friend, and one doesn't abandon one's friends easily.

I had no plan. I only knew what I had to do, not how, when, or where I would do it. With Joseph, there could be no planning. He seemed to come and go capriciously, his entrances as erratic as his appearance and personality changes, the only constant being the malice lurking beneath everything he said or did.

Ten

Jan called the next day to tell me Miriam had straightened things out with the Boone police and the Sheriff's office. "Johnny Shook was killed during the time she was at the concert with her friends."

"And that's the end of it?"

"For the police. It'll take a while for Miriam to get over it."

"You should stay with her a little longer."

"I plan to. I'll be back in a week."

The week passed with no word from Joseph, thus no opportunity for me to put my plan into action. Jan came back on a warm spring Sunday, a bright, clear day, warm when the sun was out, cool and breezy during cloudy periods. She was exhausted when I met her at Bradley International Airport, pale with large dark circles under her eyes.

"Tough week," I asked, as we left the airport parking lot.

"I hated leaving her. She's traumatized."

"She's tough."

"I know, but I can't help think she'd be better if I could stay."

"Maybe, but it can be difficult having parents around when you're her age and trying to deal with something as harrowing as this is. Did you like her friends?"

She nodded. "They've rallied around her."

"That's better than having us there picking up pieces she needs to pick up."

"I know. It's better for her. I'm not sure it's better for me."

"You're a mother."

"Forever."

"The joy and pain of having offspring."

She fell quiet; not an easy quiet, but one where she looked off into space, then at me, then back into space again, her jaw hard, her fist opening and closing. After a long sigh, she turned and leaned toward me.

"I've thought a lot about what you said before I left."

"About what?"

"That Jesus is responsible for all this. I don't appreciate it, Tommy. If you can't accept my revelation, perhaps we need to rethink things between us."

I felt the icy stab again. "I was speaking of the timing."

Her lips were thin. "Perhaps."

"Don't interpret my words."

"What else do I have to interpret?"

"Take my explanation at face value."

"I'll try."

We rode north on 91 to Greenfield without speaking, the radio tuned to the Sunday afternoon rebroadcast of *A Prairie Home Companion*. Garrison Keillor told a story about too many Lutheran ministers on a party boat. It was a rerun of an old show, but I found myself laughing at the tale even more than I had the first time I heard it. Jan remained silent.

We picked up a take-out meal and went home. Jan went to bed early, but I sat up working on my article, finally going upstairs after midnight. She was up at first light, a little before five AM. I heard her rise, but kept my eyes closed, and was soon back asleep. The digital clock said it was 7:15 when she came into the bedroom and shook me awake. I felt as though I hadn't slept.

"Charlie Mathews is dead." She sat on the edge of the bed beside me, the newspaper in her shaking hands.

Pulling myself up, I took the paper from her. The banner headline told of a late-night explosion and fire on Grove Street. Gas was responsible, the fire chief was quoted as saying, apparently from a faulty connection in the basement. The article went on to say the one fatality, Charles R. Mathews, had recently lost his wife and son in childbirth. Under the headline was a color picture of the fire, the house fully engulfed in flames.

"He never had a chance," I said. "An explosion and fire like that, hell, he must have been dead before he could stir from bed."

"That poor man," she said.

"That poor man was going to sue you for something you had no control over."

"He was distraught. I can't blame him for taking it out on me. This is awful, Tommy. How could this have happened?"

"Terrible things happen," I said. *Understand that whatever happens will be entirely on your head.* "There's no way of knowing why." *Had you not put me to this test I wouldn't have to take any action to prove myself to you.* "They just happen." *I hope something comes along to ease your wife's problems.*

"Jesus," she said. "Jesus, Jesus, Jesus Christ." Coming from anybody else, it would have sounded like a curse. I did not bring up again our talk about Jesus' responsibility.

An hour later, I drove past the ruins of the Mathews house on Grove Street. A fire truck was still there, spraying water on ashes and smoldering timbers, all that remained of the house except for a charred chimney and a cellar hole, from which more smoke rose. A group of boys stood holding their bicycles behind the yellow fire scene plastic tape, pointing at a small mound that, on closer examination, proved to be the body of a cat, its hair gone, its skin black and flaking.

"You son-of-a-bitch," I muttered. "You goddamned son-of-a-bitch." Reaching into the briefcase sitting on the seat beside me, I felt the smooth surface of my pistol. I rested my hand on it, thinking of how I had gotten to this point in my life, and reaffirmed my determination to carry out my plan, one that I now had no doubt Jan's Jesus had forced me into.

It was an exquisite irony. The son I do not believe in of a god I do not believe in had caused me to be in the position of killing a man, an act of hate and revenge that belied all the truths and values the son of that god was purported to stand for. There are those, I knew, who would comfort me by saying I was carrying out god's will. Perhaps, I thought, I would be, if he existed and was pleased by all the things men had done in his name, and in the name of the son, no matter what he had preached in his lifetime.

I sat staring at the smoldering ruins for a long time, the water from the fire hoses hissing as it hit them.

"Can you prove any of this," Bourbeau asked. He sat behind his desk, his coffee-stained white shirt open at the neck, his necktie loose around his collar. He hadn't shaved in several days.

"Joseph killed the music teacher who had been stalking my daughter, and he burned down the Mathews house to kill Charlie so he couldn't pursue the case against my wife. It's obvious," I said.

"To you, sure. To me? My boss? The DA? You gotta have evidence. What kind of facts can you give me? With what I got right now, I couldn't arrest him, even if I could find him, at least not for murder. With you as a witness, and the old lady who called it in, we could bust him for beating up on you, but that's about all we can do." He pointed a finger at me. "And, like I said, we've got to find him first. So far, you're the only person who's seen him since the incident on your street."

"He did these things to prove his friendship for me."

Bourbeau sucked his teeth. "Some people might agree that he did you a couple of favors by removing those two, the music teacher and Mathews. Some people might want to look a little more closely at you and your relationship with this guy. Some people might even think you had some connection with him doing those things."

I flushed red with anger. "Do you?"

He shrugged. "Doesn't matter. I've got no proof, not on you, not on him."

"You won't be able to prove I had a thing to do with those deaths."

He smiled, revealing teeth yellow from a lifetime of nicotine. "How many times do you figure I've heard suspects say that, and how many times do you think I've found enough evidence to put them away?"

"Am I a suspect?"

"Everybody's a suspect until we narrow a case down." He put his face in his hands, rubbing his eyes with the heels of his palms. Looking back up, he shook his head. "That doesn't mean I think you had anything to do with the murders. You're just not the type, Professor."

"I didn't think there was a type; that everyone was capable of murder."

He laughed. "Maybe in books and movies and on television cop shows, but in real life, there's people a good detective can tell in a minute are or aren't going to kill somebody. You're one of the ones who won't. Not in a million years. You don't have the stomach for it."

"I'm not so sure of that." I thought of the pistol in my briefcase, and my plans.

"Maybe, but I don't think so." He shifted in his seat. "Look, Prof, here's the best I can do. I'll have a cruiser roll by your house a couple times a night for the next week or two. If this Joseph guy comes around, pull down the window shade to the right of the front door. Maybe we'll get lucky and nab him."

The spring semester ended. I had little cause to go to campus until fall, and spent the next few days at home, working in my study on the article. Wandering around the house, I made little progress as I puttered in the small vegetable garden in the back yard and distracted myself by reading fiction. Jan was busy with her practice, often getting home after nine in the evening. We saw little of each other. When we were in the same space at the same time, we spoke only to communicate over simple matters. Are the dishes in the dishwasher clean? Is the cleaning company coming tomorrow? Did you put the trash out? Did you take your pills? Where is the unopened mayonnaise jar? Have you heard from Miriam today?

The Mohawk Trail follows Route 2 west from Greenfield through Shelburne and Charlemont to the Berkshires. Friday morning, I followed the Trail, headed to Williamstown for a long-planned visit with Brent Lewis, a friend from my undergraduate days at Amherst College. Later he had shared an apartment with Jan and me near Porter Square in Cambridge, while she was in med school and I was doing my Ph.D. It was an easy commute for them to Harvard and me to BU. Other roommates came and went, but Jan, Brent, and I made it together through the entire grueling period of graduate and med school struggles.

Brent had been teaching at Williams College since leaving Harvard. We visited back and forth several times a year, our discussions always challenging and enjoyable. I wanted to tell him about the last few months, hoping to get a rational and neutral perspective on what I had been going through.

Route 2 west between Charlemont and North Adams is a steep and twisting two-lane road winding west for miles through Savoy Mountain State Park, along the heavily wooded, dark and narrow gap separating the Pioneer Valley from the Berkshires. Stuck behind a logging truck, I watched in my rearview mirror as a blue Honda Accord with New

Hampshire plates pulled up and began to tailgate me. I tapped on my brakes, hoping my brake lights would warn the driver to back away several car lengths. He held his position and, waving at me, tooted his horn.

Veering out, I looked to see if I could pass the truck, but the curves were too close, the oncoming traffic too heavy. I pulled back into my lane, the driver of the Accord still honking and waving. I couldn't get a good look at him, but I did see long hair, a thick black beard, and dark glasses. He kept honking and waving. Ignoring him, I drove on. After two or three minutes of continued honking and waving, the driver behind me came closer and nudged my rear bumper.

I shot him the finger, regretting my action immediately. There are crazies on the roads, a large percentage of them armed. He backed away a few feet. Perhaps, I thought, he's worried about me being crazier than he and better armed. I wasn't crazy, and my gun was in the briefcase in my study. I didn't think I'd need it at staid Williams College.

At Florida, Massachusetts, the roadway straightened and leveled, with wide shoulders on each side. The Accord nudged me again, the driver pointing to the side of the road. I reached for my cell phone to call 911. No bars. I speeded up, but could go only as fast as the logging truck, and the Accord was still on my bumper, tapping it regularly, the driver pointing off toward the right shoulder. The Route 2 switchback, with its steep drop-off on the right side just before the descent into North Adams, was only a mile or two ahead. I didn't want to be driving through it with the maniac behind me, putting us both in danger, so I decided to take my chances with a confrontation.

Reaching into the back seat, I groped around until I found the steering wheel locking bar I use whenever I go to Boston and park at the Alewife garage on the Red Line. It was heavy and sturdy. Properly used, it could inflict damage on someone coming at me with violent intent.

I pulled over onto the shoulder and got out of the car, holding the lock bar at my side. The Accord parked behind me. The driver got out, and I saw immediately that the hair was a wig, the beard a fake. Only the dark glasses were real, but the combination served as a mask that barely obscured Joseph's face. He wore white painter's pants and a smock. Several artists' paint brushes stuck out of the side pocket.

"Good morning, friend," he said.

I swung the lock bar at him. He backed away, but the tip of it caught his upper left thigh, ripping his trousers and opening a slight wound.

"Nasty," he said, lunging at me with a speed I had not anticipated. Snatching the bar from my hand before I could react, he returned the blow. I looked down at a small rip in my left trouser leg, a scratch on my thigh oozing droplets of blood that ran down over my knee, staining the khakis.

He tossed me a tissue from his pocket, and took another one for himself, daubing at the blood and waving the lock bar at me each time I moved in to retrieve it. Realizing my attempts were futile, I let my hands flop at my sides, ignoring the small droplets of blood on my wound.

"I don't want to hit you with this, or with anything, Thomas."

"You've done me enough damage," I said.

"Uncle," he said.

"Uncle?"

"Do you say uncle? If so, and you can talk rationally with me, I'll dispose of this club." He waved it in front of me.

"Uncle," I sighed. There was nothing to be gained by rushing him. He'd beat me down with my own weapon, and I knew all too well the brutal violence he was capable of inflicting.

"Excellent, Thomas." He bowed, and then tossed the lock bar into the woods. Several passing cars slowed, their drivers looking at us. One, a burly man driving a red Ford F-350 with several guns on a rear window rack, pulled to a stop. Leaning across the seat, he rolled down the passenger side window.

"Your car okay, buddy," he said, looking only at me.

"Tell him everything's fine," Joseph said, his voice dark, heavy.

"If I don't?"

"He'll regret stopping, and nothing will improve for you."

"Everything's dandy," I told him.

He nodded, waved, and drove off.

"A wise move," Joseph said.

"You killed Charlie Mathews."

He looked puzzled. "Who's Charlie Mathews?"

"The man who was threatening my wife with a malpractice suit."

"And how am I supposed to have killed him?"

"In a fire last night, on Grove Street. His house burned down and he died in the fire. They've said it was due to a faulty gas line, but you did it, didn't you?"

He cocked his head. Shaking it slightly, he screwed up his face. "Charlie Mathews? That was his name? It surely was quite a fire. I was driving by when it exploded and the place burst into flames. It was beautiful." He threw his arms wide, yelled "Boom," and then added, "It was a wonderful work of art, if it wasn't an accident."

"It was no accident. You said you wanted to do something for my wife, and that whatever happened would be on my head."

"I said that?"

"Don't pretend you've forgotten."

"Perhaps I don't remember, but like I said, I did see the fire."

"And a man died in it, a man who'd already lost everyone he loved."

He lowered his head and moved it sideways. "Life is unfair, Thomas. You never know when everything is going to blow up in your face."

"You just happened to be driving on Grove Street in Greenfield in the small hours of the morning?"

"Quite a coincidence, don't you think?"

"A coincidence, you say?"

He nodded. "Do you know anything about Cai Guo-Qiang?"

"Never heard of it, and what's it got to do with any of this?"

"Not it, him. Cai is an artist who works in paint and gunpowder. He'll make a painting using both, and when it's finished, he ignites the gunpowder. The results are amazing. He also does explosion events. It all has to do with the processes of the destruction and transformation of life. The pure force of energy as art. What happened to your friend's house last night looked like a work of Cai's art. One minute it was standing there on the street, looking like any one of the other houses lined up on either side of it. Then in an instant it was transformed. I suppose your friend was equally transformed. Static forms became kinetic, bursting and flaming into their elemental components. The entire life process in a twinkling. Boom. Swish. Flump."

"And you were the artist?"

"I don't care to believe I was, Thomas."

I took a deep breath, held it for as long as possible, and then expelled it slowly, flapping my lips as I did. It helped control my trembling.

"You once told me your employer was a god of vengeance. What did that mean, and who is he?"

He leaned against the hood of his car, laughing and shaking his head. "You must have imagined that. I don't make such overblown statements. I have no employer, Thomas, unless it's my regard for you, and as for a god of vengeance, I don't believe in gods, devils, angels, demons, or any other kind of supernatural crap. Nor do you, I suppose. Let me assure you, I don't believe I would have said something so ridiculously inane."

"You did."

"There's just no accounting, is there?"

I walked backwards toward my car. I opened the door, resting my palms on its top.

"I'm getting in the car and leaving now. If you keep following me, I'll call the police as soon as I can get cell service."

"I can tell when I'm not wanted, Thomas. We'll continue this talk next time."

"Next time I see you, I will kill you." I spoke with as much quiet and calm as I could muster.

"Oh Thomas, you won't do that." He waved his hand dismissively through the air. "Killing me, killing anybody, isn't your style, and it wouldn't solve anything for you. Oh, you'd be rid of me, certainly, but all the other problems of your life would remain. I'm not your nemesis, nor am I the source of your problems, just as Charlie Mathews wasn't your wife's real problem, or Johnny Shook your daughter's."

"Killing you would give me extreme pleasure."

"No, Thomas, it wouldn't. You would mourn me the remainder of your days."

"I doubt that."

I got in my car and started the motor. He leaned in the open window. "I didn't start that fire, Thomas. But you're glad it happened, aren't you?"

Pulling onto Route 2 without replying, I saw him recede in my rearview mirror, standing by the roadside, hands on his hips, watching until I rounded the next bend. I didn't see him again as I drove west towards Williamstown.

Brent Lewis was in his office. Tall, clean shaven, his long hair gray and falling to his shoulders. He wore faded jeans and a plain, navy blue t-shirt.

"Holy shit," he said, pointing at my eye patch. "What happened?"

I told him about Jan's declaration of faith, described Joseph's appearances in my life, and the deaths of Johnny Shook and Charlie Mathews, and concluded by describing my encounter with Joseph on Route 2.

He grunted in disbelief. "Are you going to be all right, Tommy?"

"I suppose." I fingered the patch. "Actually, I'm a wreck, but I can't let Jan or anybody else in my daily circle see that I'm totally fucked up. My vision is flat."

"What can I do?"

"Listen. Maybe give me some sage advice."

"I don't have any. It sounds like you've taken every reasonable step there is, and they haven't led anywhere."

"So tell me to kill the fucker."

He squinted his eyes. "Kill the fucker?"

"Say it without the question mark."

"Kill the fucker."

"Thanks."

"Don't. I was just following your orders to drop the Q mark."

"It's what I wanted to hear."

"You're not going to do it?"

"Now don't drop the question mark."

He looked out the window before changing the subject. "Miriam's in Boone, you say? What's she doing there?"

"Teaching at the high school."

"Kenny Byrd used to teach philosophy at Appalachian State, you know. We keep in touch. I visited him last summer. He's living out in the woods in a log shack he built in Sugar Grove, about ten miles west of Boone."

"Who's Kenny Byrd?"

He gave me a strange look. "Byrd was that philosophy grad student who rented the extra bedroom next to the kitchen our third year in Porter Square. He was a lunatic, always talking about the necessity for man to be free from restraints on his ability to do anything to preserve his well-being, however he chose to define well-being, even if it meant killing somebody. Don't you remember? He had all that NRA literature that he passed out on the street, and stuff from the John Birch Society and the Ayn Rand fanatics? Jesus, people used to get so pissed off at him, and the University tried to boot him out of the Ph.D. program until he got the ACLU after them."

"I don't remember him. Maybe it was after I left."

"No way. I left the same time you did."

I shook my head.

"I can't believe you've forgotten him. You and Jan tried to get Peter Glick and me to agree to throw him out, and Peter insisted that we had to be open to all kinds of ideas, even if they made us puke. It was the only way, he said, that we could claim to have any intellectual integrity."

"What happened?"

"He left anyway. After the civil liberties people scared the University into backing off, he told his advisor to go fuck himself, and quit the program."

"But you said he was teaching philosophy at Appalachian. You need a doctorate to do that."

"He transferred to Princeton. He was a right wing crazy, but he wasn't stupid. Princeton's more sympathetic to those types. We all went out to dinner to celebrate his leaving. You even offered a toast to him, wishing him good luck."

"I don't remember any of that."

"Kenny remembers you. I talked to him on the phone last week, and he asked about you, wondering how you were coping."

I was confused. "He said that, how was I coping?"

Brent nodded. He frowned. "You do remember Peter?"

"Sure. He wrote his dissertation on women troubadours in Provence, and then went to law school. He's a Republican lobbyist in DC."

"Well fuck him," Brent said.

"Right. With a corn cob dipped in rubbing alcohol."

We both laughed.

"You really don't remember Kenny? He was from the Carolina mountains, a place with a funny name, Little Switzerland. I remember, when he told us about his home town, thinking it sounded made up, like a tourist promotion, not the kind of name you'd expect a hillbilly town to have. Not like Pigeon Roost, 'Tater Gap, Beech Creek, Sugar Grove, Elmer's Holler, something like that."

"Don't say hillbilly. That's like the N word for mountain people."

'Sorry. I forgot that Jan's from down there."

"I can't recall any Benny Byrd."

"Kenny."

"He might as well have never existed."

"Ask his neighbors if he exists. He runs moonshine, shoots at tin cans and bottles, groundhogs, porcupines and, maybe even at dogs and cats, blasting away with a 30.06. Sometimes, they say, until the middle of the night. He spooks the hell out of the locals, waking them up at all hours with his guns, sometimes with his stereo turned up so loud it rattles their roofs, according to one old man down the road from him. I asked at the general store how to find his place, and the woman said, 'you mean Unabomber, Jr.?' When I said yes, she wouldn't tell me anything else, just lowered her eyes and started fidgeting with things on the shelves. I finally found him by going to the post office. A woman at the counter didn't want to tell me anything, until I told her I was from the FBI."

"She didn't ask for identification?"

He laughed. "She just looked tickled to think she was talking to a fellow Fed, and told me everything I wanted to know. Kenny's got quite the reputation. She leaned over the counter, made sure no one else could hear her, and told me she was sure he was growing marijuana out there, and that he probably had a meth lab, too."

"Did he?"

"Not that I could see. He's whacked out, and must have close to a hundred guns hanging on the walls, over the windows and doors, three of them over the fireplace, and a bunch of them lined up in cabinets in his bedroom: enough to hold off a siege."

"Who'd lay siege to him?"

"I don't think he's afraid of the DEA."

"What do you think he's afraid of?"

"Who knows? Life? The Establishment? Mormon missionaries? Encyclopedia salesmen?" He paused, and then continued with a serious look. "My guess would be life. He left Appalachian on pretty nasty terms. He didn't talk much about it, but from what he said, he was pretty bitter. He said his department chair told a bunch of lies to deny him tenure. He appealed, but it was turned down. There was a newspaper photograph of a man on the wall over the stove, and there must have been ten darts in his face. I asked who he was, and Kenny said the president of the University."

"You're sure he asked about me, asked how I was coping?"

"As sure as I am that I'm talking with you right now."

"Did he say what he thought I was coping with?"

"Nope. I asked him what he meant, and he told me to forget it. He was just asking about you in general, he said, and that we all have to cope with aging."

"What else did he say about me, beyond asking how I was coping?"

"That was it."

"And you say I wanted him out of our apartment back in Cambridge?"

"That's how I remember it. Since he was asking about you and wondering how you were coping, I'd assume he doesn't remember it that way, or hold any grudge against you if he does."

I closed my eyes and tried envisioning the apartment. I could see the room next to the kitchen, the smallest of the bedrooms we had, and we had rented it out to several students during the time we leased the place. I remember one in particular, Harold Levy, a short, wiry, black belt who was working toward an MBA at Northeastern. He stayed in the room for six months before leaving to move in with his girlfriend. There was Betsy Allen, there for eight months, and J. Randolph Monroe, who we kicked out after five weeks of putting up with his drugs and druggie friends. But I had no recollection of a Kenny Byrd. I didn't believe Brent was having me on, but what other answer could there be to my drawing a total blank when trying to conjure up the slightest hint of a memory that might even touch on him? It was unsettling.

"Nothing, nada, zip. There's no Kenny Byrd in my memory banks."

Brent gave me an odd look, then spoke as one might speak to a child, or an old person in the early stages of dementia. "You were pretty busy back then. We called you The Grind, they way you worked as a local political stringer for that suburban paper at night, and studied whenever you weren't in class during the day."

"The seeds for all my political theories lie in local politics. What a mess they were. And I was pretty busy back then. We all were. Looking back, it almost seems that Jan and I had sex less then, in our most fecund days, than we do now in our early geezerdom."

He grunted again. "It's odd you don't remember Kenny. You were pretty worked up over him back in those days."

"Busy or not, you'd think I'd remember a character like that, especially if he agitated me enough to lobby for throwing him out of the apartment."

"You'd think so," Brent said.

"It can't be Alzheimer's. That's when you can't make new memories, but can still dig up the old ones."

"Supposedly."

"So I'm either nuts, or you're lying."

"Or you've just forgotten."

"Or that."

We fell into a long silence. Outside his open window we could hear the sounds of the campus, the roar of mowers, the voices of summer school students playing Frisbee on the lawn, wind rustling the leaves on nearby trees. Brent spoke first.

"How about them Red Sox."

"How about them," I said. "They've even welcomed Billy Buckner back to town."

We chuckled, and talked about Buckner's tenth inning error in game six against the Mets in the 1986 World Series, which Boston led three games to two. A line drive down first base went through his legs, costing the Sox the game and ultimately the series.

"It was cool the way the Sox had him toss out the first pitch at their home opener this year. The fans gave him a four minute standing ovation," Brent said.

"You just never know what's going to happen. He'd been a good player over the years. He just had a bad day, and it colored the rest of his life."

"They'd still be ignoring him if they hadn't won last year and in 2004."

The conversation drifted to increasingly trivial topics, before ending in another long silence. When Brent stretched and sighed, looking toward his computer screen, I knew it was time to leave.

Emerging from his office building into the bright sun, I stood and looked over the perfectly manicured lawns of the Williams campus. Bisected by Route 2, they slope gently north, down to the Hoosic River, the hills of southern Vermont just two miles away. The care with which the campus is maintained, and the almost artistic arrangement of its buildings in juxtaposition to one another, provide the impression of order and successful planning so essential to the academic illusion, and stand in dramatic contrast to the U-Mass campus, with its ungainly buildings, an unattractive mixture of new and old, the worst of public university architecture and planning, placed in no particular pattern in relationship to each other. Perhaps that's why I have stayed there all these years, taking some pride in the University's apparent lack of an overall design.

It is my metaphor.

Eleven

"Do you remember Kenny Byrd," I asked Jan the following morning. We were in the kitchen having coffee with ham and cheese croissants, which I had picked up earlier at the co-op when I went for my *New York Times*. Things between us were still strained, but casual civil conversations were again possible.

Jan chuckled lightly. "What a pain he was. You and I politicked for weeks before we got Brent and Peter to agree to evict him, and then before we could tell him he was out, he told us he was transferring to Princeton."

"I don't remember."

"Kenny, or his transferring?"

"Any of it."

She furrowed her brow. "Do you feel all right?"

"I feel fine."

"Never confused about where you are, or how to get home?"

"Of course not."

"Who's the President of the United States?" She was grinning at me.

"Stop. My memory's intact, I don't have problems making coffee or keeping my check book balanced. I can find my way back and forth to work. I give coherent lectures to my classes, even if some of the undergraduates are too dense to follow them."

Waving her hands in the air, her eyes crinkled in a smile. "You're as sound as anyone I know, but you have to admit, it's weird that you don't remember Kenny."

"It's not weird to me. If I suddenly did remember him and remembered not remembering, that might seem a little peculiar."

"He was a strange kid."

"According to Brent, he's an even stranger man."

Jan took a bite from her croissant. Watching her chew, her eyes looking from side to side, her lips occasionally parting enough for me to see her teeth, I was struck by a sense of the dominance of our animal qualities. It was not a new realization. It is one I often glimpse and then deny, preferring to think instead of us in our humanness, our humanity.

My ruined eye was aching, my good one watering. The flat world of my vision was wavering from fluid distortion, and sunlight streaming through the windows was magnified in its brilliance. A sharp pain pierced my head. With an involuntary gasp and groan, I jerked upright. My body shook, and I was stunned by a bright and sudden light as everything went white. My jaw clenched tight, the room spun, and I lost consciousness.

"Are you all right," Jan asked. "You passed out for about twenty seconds." She was hovering over me, holding my head firmly between her hands.

I heard my voice mumble, "I don't know." My tongue was sore, my lips wet. I wiped them with the back of my hand, and it came away covered with blood. "What happened," I asked her.

"We're going to find out."

Five hours later, Bob Shedd—a neurologist with a practice in Jan's office building—stood over my gurney in the ER. "Good news. All the tests were normal. You're fine, Tommy."

My socket was still painful. "What happened?"

"You had a seizure, and I'm not sure why. Sometimes the brain just short circuits, and it never happens again. I don't think you need worry too much. It was a small episode, maybe an aftereffect of the beating you took, but nothing showed up in the EEG or the scans. Your cognition is good. You don't seem confused, and all your other vital signs are fine. I'm going to send you home." He looked at Jan. "Just keep an eye on him for the next few hours."

"I don't feel fine," I said. I remembered how I had passed out in my office, the day Joseph had taken me to his bunker, and how the world had seemed to deteriorate into an atmosphere breaking apart, filled with holes. Not wanting to subject myself to more tests and a possible hospitalization, I did not mention it.

"Trust me," he said. "You're going to be all right."

"I don't even trust myself."

"I can't help you with that. I'm a neurologist, not a shrink. If you have any more of these seizures, that's when we'll have to worry."

"Perhaps you're like Saul on the road to Damascus," Jan said once Bob was gone.

"I saw the light. It was just light."

She rested her hand on my head. "Perhaps."

Bourbeau called a few hours later. I was resting on the couch, watching the newsmouths speculate about the outcome of the day's Montana and South Dakota primaries.

"I got a body I want you to look at over at the hospital morgue."

"Anybody I know?"

"That's what I want to find out. Could be your friend Joseph."

"That would be nice. My birthday's next week."

"Maybe we can wrap things up for you," he said.

"I don't think you should drive," Jan said, when I told her about Bourbeau's request.

"I'm okay. I don't have a trace of pain or visual disturbance left. Besides, the hospital's only three blocks away. I'd walk if it weren't raining."

Bourbeau and Novak were waiting for me in the hallway outside the morgue.

"You sure it's Joseph," I asked.

"Think we'd ask you down if we was sure," Novak said.

"Thanks for coming," Bourbeau said, giving Novak a sharp look, surreptitiously poking him in the ribs with a forefinger.

The body was in a zippered bag lying on a gurney. A cardboard box sat on the floor beside it.

"Before we view the deceased, I want you to look at his things." Bourbeau overturned the box on an adjacent gurney. The pile included a camel hair overcoat, stained with mud and a dark crust I assumed was blood, a crushed tan fedora, a shirt, underpants, a pair of shoes heavy with mud, and a pair of filthy white socks.

"Nothing else," I asked. "No wallet, nothing to identify him?"

"Just this crap and the corpse, and that ain't a pretty thing," Novak said. "For one thing, he's been dead a while, and for another, whoever killed him didn't like him very much. They messed him up real bad, and nobody's cleaned him up yet."

Bourbeau said, "We ran his fingerprints, did DNA, the works. Nothing came up. The guy's a cipher."

Novak looked from Bourbeau to me. "The boss here wants you to see him raw. Got a clothespin for your dainty Tuckerman Court nose?"

"Enough," Bourbeau said.

Novak unzipped the body bag. The odor was strong, but mixed with antiseptic and a room deodorant, and with my nostrils buried in my right hand, it was not unbearable. I looked down at the body. The face was bloodied and disfigured by a number of blows to the head. He looked as though someone had battered him with a sledge hammer. The forehead was caved in and broken, bits of brain tissue showing through shattered bone. One eye was missing, the other unrecognizable. He did have a heavy mustache, the type Joseph had the day he and Randy came after me. It was hard to tell what kind of eyebrows he'd had.

"That him," Novak asked.

"I don't know."

"Look again." Bourbeau's voice was soft, and he rested his hand on my shoulder.

"Was he wearing those?" I pointed to the clothes.

"He was naked. They were in a pile next to the body."

I leaned over and studied the face. With the mustache it could have been Joseph as he looked that day, but not as I had seen him since then. "Where did you find him?"

"Some kids playing with their dogs in Highland Park found him off the trail by the high tension lines."

"Freaked them out," Novak said with a brief snort of a laugh. "They'll be waking up with nightmares when they're in their forties. The beating isn't what killed him, though." He unzipped the bag further, and pointed to a wound on the left side of the corpse's chest. "That's what finished him, poor fucker, stabbed right in the heart."

Bourbeau said, "He'd been there at least three days."

"It can't be Joseph," I said.

Novak jutted his chin, smacking his hands together. "Those are the right clothes, just like you described, and the mustache, like you said."

"I saw Joseph yesterday, out on Route 2 west of Charlemont."

"You sure," Novak asked.

"I'm not stupid," I told him.

"Course not," he said. "You're a perfessor, right?"

"Cool it, Sy," Bourbeau said, turning to me. "This is the first time I've heard about yesterday. Why didn't you file a report?"

"Why tell you anything, since you don't have the resources to follow up?"

He blew out, rattling his lips. "We're stretched thin, for sure."

"Looks to me as if someone wanted you to think it was Joseph, so they beat him beyond an easy identification and left his clothes, or clothes like his, there to throw you off. I'd wager that Joseph did it."

"Or you could be lying about seeing him yesterday," Novak said.

"Why would I do that?"

"Because you killed him," he said.

"I'm not a killer." There was a tremor in my voice and my heart was racing. A hot flush ran up my neck and into my cheeks.

"All killers say they're not killers." Novak's chin was like a knife pointed at me. Bourbeau remained silent.

I saw their game and backed off. Let them talk. I had done nothing, and I had nothing to say beyond my earlier suggestion that Joseph killed whoever was lying on the gurney, that he found someone resembling the way he looked the day he and Randy attacked me, killed him, maiming the face to make identification difficult, and left the clothes there to clinch things. There was no point in repeating it. Doing so would make me look overly anxious to convince them of my innocence.

"You can't give us a positive ID," Bourbeau finally asked, his tone resigned.

"It can't be Joseph. Like I told you, I saw him yesterday and talked to him. Even were it he, I couldn't make a positive identification. The time he and Randy beat me I was seeing in three dimensions. Now I see in two. That flattens the features, changes my vision, the way the world appears."

Novak expelled another of his unpleasant snorts. "*Even were it he.* Jesus, Lenny, ain't the perfesser got fancy shmancy ways of talking. He's fucking lying. Three dimensions and two dimensions. Bullshit. If he can't see right, how come he's driving a car?"

I had a fleeting desire to dig my thumbs into both his eyes and push his jutting little jaw into a shattered mass at the back of this throat.

"Maybe you should talk to someone at the Registry of Motor Vehicles about it," Bourbeau told him. Novak seem pleased by the idea, and made a notation on a small pad of paper he took from his pocket.

"You can go, Professor Rutherford. Thanks for coming down." Bourbeau said to me. He looked at Novak. "Put the clothes back in the box, and make sure things are taken care of down here."

I nodded, and without a word, left the morgue. Novak stared at me as he stood motionless beside the naked body on the gurney.

Bourbeau followed me down the hall to the elevator. "If that is Joseph, and you did kill him, I wouldn't blame you."

"It's not, and I didn't."

He tightened his lips. "We'll get an ID on the body one way or another. I'll call you as soon as we do."

"Why would you call me if you think I might have killed him?"

"If it is this Joseph guy, I don't know if you killed him. You're a suspect, a main suspect, but my gut tells me you're not a killer. Novak's gut tells him you are." He shrugged. "We each see a different man when we look at you, but it doesn't matter what either one of us thinks. We just present what we get to the DA, and she'll make a decision. If it looks like she's going to go for an indictment, I'll call to give you a heads up, so you'll have time to get a lawyer lined up before a load of shit lands on you."

"You do that for all your suspects?"

"Just those that I'm sure aren't going to run away."

"I've got no need to."

"I hope not."

The elevator door opened, and I stepped inside. He was still standing in the hall, his eyes on mine as it closed.

Back home, I filled a shopping bag with tin cans, took my briefcase, and went across the Connecticut to the Turners Fall Rod and Gun Club on the river's edge. Setting the cans in various spots on the rifle range, I plinked away at them with the Smith and Wesson. I grazed some, sending them skittering across the dirt. Others I hit square, ripping them open. Each was Joseph's heart. Delighted by the sounds of my modified hollow points making contact with the cans, I shot up a full box of rounds.

Done, I sat on a rock watching the river flow by, and cleaned the pistol. Loading a final six rounds into the revolver, I engaged the safety and returned it to my briefcase. It was late in the day, the sun pale and the shadows long. The afternoon had been hot, and I relaxed in a cool breeze blowing from the water. People paddled by in red, blue, orange, and yellow kayaks, their voices carrying to my perch. In the age-old tradition of nautical courtesy, most paddlers waved to me. I waved back, envious of their easy laughter and song.

Uncomfortable after a while, I moved from the rock to the grass, to the picnic benches by the club house. The sight of the body in the morgue preyed on me. It could not have been Joseph, but the resemblance its broken features bore to his, even to my one eye, was startling. Novak clearly wanted me for the murder, and he was Bourbeau's tool, playing the heavy to upset me and render me careless. Had I been guilty of the murder, it might have worked.

I stayed there until well after dark, kayaks and other boats gone, the river quiet save for the sound of water brushing the banks and breaking over boulders jutting up along its course.

My cell phone rang.

"Where are you," Jan asked.

"I'll be home soon."

"You're all right?"

"I'm fine."

"I was worried."

"I'm really okay."

"Come home." I could hear the worry in her voice.

"Be there in a few minutes."

"Hurry," she said, the worry rising.

Driving up Tuckerman Court, I realized how self absorbed I had been since my first encounter with Joseph and Randy. Jan was being tossed around as well. Whatever the source and meaning of her Jesus thing, it was important to her, and stood in stark opposition to her strong early convictions, ones that I had never doubted until that late day in March. Perhaps it was a sign of emotional or intellectual deterioration, perhaps it came from a deeply felt and genuine spiritual revelation, perhaps they were one and the same. No matter which, it was time for me to attend to her.

She sat on the porch steps. I walked from the car to the house, and she rose to meet me, giving me a clinging hug.

"Hey," she said.

"Hi." I buried my face in her hair, breathing deeply of its rich oily smell.

"I was afraid something had happened to you."

"Everything's fine." I told her about the body, and Bourbeau and Novak's suspicions. I did not mention the pistol in the briefcase at my side, nor my time on the Turners Falls shooting range.

"Could it have been Joseph," she asked.

"I don't see how." I described the incident on the Trail. "Are you all right," I concluded.

"I'm wonderful."

I kissed her neck. "Of course you are. You've always been wonderful, as far as I can see."

Drawing away she giggled, a sound I had not heard from her in a long time. "Silly, I mean I feel wonderful. Of course it's terrible about Mimi and the Shook boy, and what happened to you and having that horrible Joseph man following you around, and the tragedy of the Mathews family, but with Jesus reassuring me every day, I take them in stride and keep looking forward, going forward. I'm not sure I could have done any of that without him."

"Do you still say you're not a Christian?"

"My relationship with Jesus is one on one. I don't need a church, a preacher, hymns, or prayers. He reaches out to me and I reach out to him. I especially don't need preachers. I had enough of them around me back in Banner Elk, pompous self-serving hypocrites, most of them. I may not be a Christian, but I am Christ-centered. The church is not. Not any church."

"We used to be able to reassure each other every day, and keep looking and going forward as a result." As soon as I spoke, I wished I could have taken the words back, in tone if not in content. They were not what I had in mind when I decided to attend to her.

Her reply was gracious. "We still do, or we can. My relationship with Jesus isn't a substitute for our relationship, any more than my relationships with my friends and colleagues are substitutes."

"How did it happen, this relationship with Jesus?" The word relationship was not uttered gently, and I had another moment of regret, and she had another moment of grace.

"I don't know, Tommy. It's like I told you before, how it had been building in me, and how it was so overwhelming that I couldn't talk about it until it was full born." She stopped for a moment and looked out at the street, toward the spot where I had been lying after Joseph and Randy finished with me. Turning her gaze back to me, she sighed, a deep insuck of breath followed by a long exhalation, inspiration followed by expiration.

"Funny I should have used the words full born," she said with a faint smile. "I've participated in so many births that they'd become a mechanical process for me to oversee. I'd lost the wonder of it all, and I've done so many abortions that I've come to regard all life from that same mechanistic perspective, something to be manipulated, not something to be in awe of."

I could not keep the alarm out of my voice. "Don't tell me you've become a right to lifer?"

She laughed out loud, a long and unreserved sound. "Of course I haven't. Women have an inborn right to control their reproductive lives." She looked at me. "There's that word again, and I'll use it in another way: woman have borne too much over the course human history—and they still are in benighted areas of the world—to ever again have the most intimate and private aspects of our lives controlled by somebody other than ourselves."

"Does Jesus agree?"

"He does."

"How do you know?"

"He speaks to me, answers my questions, and soothes my doubts. He's restored the wonder to my world."

"It must be nice to have such certainty."

"It's difficult. I have to reaffirm it every moment. I have to constantly renew my faith and know that I'm not a whack job, that I'm not hearing voices and deceiving myself. People who hear voices are often crazy. There are volumes filled with diagnoses for them." She led me to the porch steps, and we sat down. I rested the briefcase near my feet. Her gaze returned to the spot on the street, and my own followed. "I'm not crazy, Tommy."

It was not a statement inflected as a question. It was an affirmation, strong, and brooking no denial. The breeze that had been blowing earlier down by the river had become a wind, one that promised rain. In the light of the streetlamps, I saw leaves on the maples along Tuckerman Court turn their silvery sides upward.

"You're not crazy." I held her hand and played with her fingers. "But you have to admit, all this might be a delusion resulting from too much work, too much stress. Your job is tough, demanding in so many ways. Like all docs, you lose people, and that must make you doubt yourself. Jesus could be a defense mechanism, protecting you, giving you a shield from the pain and burdens of your work."

She did not jerk away, remove her hand from mine, or lash out with words. She simply shook her head and replied in a calm and bemused voice. "It's no delusion, Tommy. I love you, and I love the way you just tried to talk sense into me without attacking, but I'm in full possession of my senses and my faculties. I am not deluded. My Jesus is real. He is in my heart, and he speaks to me in ways that are enlightening."

"Jesus as the light? That's very neo-platonic," I said.

She laughed. "No theology, Tommy. It's just Jesus and me."

"And me?" I realized I sounded jealous.

"And you. Has my love for Miriam ever detracted from my love for you?"

"We haven't always had as much time for each other as we did before she came along, but that's all right. There was more love to go around. I didn't love you less because she was there, I just loved her, too, and I love you more because of it."

"Exactly." There was triumph in her voice.

I sat back, resting my elbows on the step above me. "I'm hungry."

"Trying to change the subject?"

"No. I'm hungry."

After a brief discussion of what we didn't have in the refrigerator, I volunteered to go to the co-op and pick up food from their hot table.

"Nothing with cilantro," Jan said. "I can drink dish detergent if that's the flavor I'm looking for."

"If Bourbeau calls, take a message. He said he'd let me know if they could identify the body in the morgue. He thinks it's Joseph."

"You don't?"

"How could it be? I've seen him since the John Doe's estimated time of death."

Ten minutes later, outside the co-op, a heavyset middle-aged man detached himself from a group of other men who sat at the outside tables and on the sidewalk around them, taking turns drinking from a bottle poorly concealed in a brown paper bag. He wore a t-shirt with several holes in the shoulders and a Greenfield Community College baseball cap. His dungarees were ripped and dirty, and his feet were encased in sandals that looked as if they were about to fall apart. Thinking he was going to hit me up for beer money, I avoided his eyes and reached for the door.

"Hey," he said, putting out a hand with fingernails yellowed and thick with fungus. A wad of chewing gum framed by long canines moved around in the open area where his top front teeth had once been. "You were one of my favorite professors at U-Mass."

I tried to see the young student he might once have been, but didn't recognize him. "I've forgotten your name," I said.

"Fred Pratt," he said. "I was in your Constitutional law class in '91." His hand was still out, I awkwardly shook it. "You were a major influence on me."

"What are you doing now, Fred?" His name stirred a dim memory of a kid with strong political convictions, eager to understand how things were stacked in the political world so that he might work to make the world a better place.

"I'm a drunk." He spoke as if drunkenness were a profession, with as little emotion as he might have told me he was a bus driver or a social worker. "You remember that paper I wrote on how Reagan fucked up the Supreme Court?"

"I'm sorry, Fred, but I've read a lot of papers during my career. I don't think I could dredge up a memory of something you wrote seventeen years ago."

His eyes hard on mine, he recited a paragraph. It was concise and insightful. "You don't remember that," he asked.

I shook my head, wondering how and why he had memorized it.

"How about this?" He closed his eyes and started a sentence that deteriorated into gibberish, a string of sounds that rhymed but were not words. "Remember that?"

"Sorry," I said, and reached out to shake his hand again. "I've got to run. My wife's waiting for me to bring something home for dinner."

"I never married," he said. "The world's too fucked up."

"Take care," I said, and ducked into the store. Looking through the window, I saw him rejoin the circle of drinkers, take the bag, and lift it to his lips for a long time, the others hooting at him and reaching for the bottle.

He was leaving when I came back out. I saw him disappear into an alley with a smaller man, both lurching, their arms around one another's shoulders. Fred passed him the brown bag just as they disappeared from sight.

Often I meet former students in stores, on the streets of Greenfield and Amherst, and even, on occasion, in Northampton and Brattleboro, Vermont. I have forgotten most of them, although I've become as smooth as a politician in smiling, telling them how good it is to see them again and asking after their post-University lives. Fred Pratt's question is a common one: remember that paper, remember that time in class, remember how you told me, remember that girl who sat in the front row, remember remember remember?

I rarely do.

I sat in my car, parked in the driveway, depressed by my encounter with Fred Pratt and reluctant to go in the house. The wind was blowing ever harder, rocking the car, but the rain was holding off. Jan would be waiting, dishes on the table, probably a bottle of Cote de Rhone open and breathing on the kitchen counter. CNN would be on the kitchen TV, a newsmouth droning about Obama and Hillary's secret meeting the night before in Washington, spouting imaginary scenarios of what might have happened between the two of them, why he would or would not, why she would or would not, agree on what the newsmouths in general referred to as the dream ticket, a phrase that had taken on a life of its own.

After several minutes, stirring myself from what was almost a stupor, I carried the food inside. The TV was on. I set the bag on the counter next to the wine, and looked at the screen. The analyst of the moment, a political whore with a comb-over hair who has served as an advisor to presidents of both parties, never to their advantage, was explaining, emphatically, why Obama would not ever put Hillary on the ticket as his running mate, ever... unless he did. He was followed by another pundit—a failed Republican presidential candidate from several electoral cycles past—who just as emphatically countered with why Obama would of course put Hillary on the ticket as his running mate... unless he didn't.

"Had enough of this," I asked Jan, picking up the remote.

"More than enough."

I clicked it off.

"Nobody knows diddly, do they," she said.

"And they sound so adamant about it." I put the food on plates. It was a simple dinner, two garlic chicken thighs apiece, a small pile of roasted rosemary potatoes, and some steamed spinach.

Jan poured us each a glass of wine. It was a Cote de Rhone. Handing one to me, she gave me an exaggerated wink. "Hey sailor, want to go upstairs with me after dinner and see if we can make things work?"

"Ahoy," I said.

Twelve

I would see Joseph one more time.

Waking at three in the morning to a clap of thunder and brilliant lightning, I rolled over and looked at Jan. She had a pillow over her head, her snores muffled and regular. There was a second clap, louder than the first. She groaned and turned onto her side. Emerging from a deep sleep, she breathed irregularly. The rain was heavy and loud on the tin roof of the porch outside our bedroom window. Rising, I pulled the curtains aside and looked out.

"You getting up," she muttered.

"Just for a minute."

Through the rain-streaked night air I saw an unfamiliar car parked beneath the streetlamp. Its windows were steamed, as if someone were inside it, watching the house. I put on a robe and went downstairs, turning on the hall light as I did. When I stepped out onto the porch, the car was gone. The asphalt where it had been sitting was as wet as the rest of the pavement.

Jan came out on the porch and stood beside me. "What are you doing here?"

"There was a car parked out front."

"Probably the police," she said.

"It didn't look like a police car."

"Who else could it be?" After a pause she said, "Joseph?"

"That's what I'm afraid of."

"Well, he's gone now."

"I hope so."

She shivered and took my arm, pulling me back into the house. "I'm afraid, Tommy."

"Why? Won't Jesus protect you?" I touched her hand. "I'm sorry. That was uncalled for."

"It doesn't work that way. Things still happen, bad as well as good. Jesus is comfort, a solace, a way of knowing, a way of being. He's not a comic book superhero or a cop. He doesn't protect us from the bad things in the world. He helps us cope with them."

"I have my own ways of coping," I said, glancing over at the briefcase sitting on the dining room table.

We sat in the kitchen, drinking milk and eating crackers and cheese. The rain grew heavier, and several long rolls of thunder lasted for minutes at a time, lightning flashing constantly.

"Aren't you frightened," she asked. There was a peal of thunder I could feel in my chest, followed by a brilliant flash of lightning. The electric sockets sparked, and we both jumped. "I don't mean of the storm. I mean of Joseph."

I shook my head. I was, but I didn't want to talk about it, and I especially didn't want to discuss it with her. Anything I could say would only ratchet her fear up to another level. "Let's go back to bed," I said.

We went upstairs. She snuggled close to me, her head on my shoulder, my arm around her. Soon she was asleep. We lay there until first light, when I eased my arm from beneath her, and went to my study to work on the article.

At ten after seven, a message popped up on my computer screen. *Friend,* it said. *We need to talk. Can you meet me for breakfast?*

No, I typed in response. *You know where you can stuff your breakfast.*

The words, *Not very nice. Not very smart,* appeared quickly.

What were you doing parked outside my house in the middle of the night?

Moi? Thomas, why would I do that?

That was my question.

Ask me again at breakfast.

No breakfast. We have nothing to discuss.

Not very nice. Not very smart, came on the screen again.

I logged off and shut down the computer.

The newspaper came late. I was still reading it, drinking coffee, and munching on a bagel, when Jan came downstairs at 8:30, dressed for work in gray slacks and a blue blouse, a white lab coat over them. She poured some coffee into a silver thermos.

"I'm late for a meeting with the malpractice lawyer from the insurance company."

"I thought that was all over with Charlie Mathews' death."

"There's still paperwork. Beside, there could be some heirs who might want to go on with the case."

"Are there?"

She took a large bite of my bagel, crumbs falling on her chest. "I don't know," she mumbled with her mouth full.

"I'm sorry. I thought that was one stressor we could put behind you."

"I'm fine." Her voice was bright, untroubled.

Planting a quick kiss on my cheek, she left me in the kitchen. I heard her fumbling around in the dining room, collecting her things, and then the front door opened and closed, and she was gone. I looked out into the back yard. The storm had passed. The clouds were breaking up, and streaks of sunlight shone through the trees.

I considered my options for the day. I could go to the University, do research in the library for my article. I could work in the office, organizing my courses for the fall semester, and risk running into R.C. Alexander. I could pack a lunch, hike the High Ledges, and find a picnic spot overlooking the Deerfield Valley. I could stay home, hide in my study, and pretend to work on the article, but I would get little accomplished without further research, and I would be distracted by the many chores Jan had on her list of Things That Need To Get Done Soon, things I too often manage to forget or put off indefinitely. I could get roaring drunk and pass out on the front porch couch.

I decided on the High Ledges. I made a peanut butter sandwich and wrapped three beers in an ice pack Jan keeps in the freezer for treating the various injuries we are prone to in our late middle age—early old age, she calls it. I put them in a paper bag and started for the door. Halfway there I stopped, took the Smith and Wesson from the briefcase, and stuck it in the bag with my lunch. The phone rang as I was opening the front door. Unwilling to talk to anyone, especially Joseph, I waited for the answering machine to kick in. It was Miriam.

"Hey, Daddy," she said when I picked up. "Do you remember a Ken Byrd?"

"I don't, although Brent tells me I should."

"He called me this morning. He wanted to know how I was, and said he was worried about you. He asked me how you were coping."

"Coping with what, did he say?"

"That's all he said, just asked how you were coping, and said I should call you and say he sent his best."

"Did he tell you why he didn't call me himself?"

"He just said I should call. Daddy, he sounds like a wicked weird guy. He talked in a half whisper, and said 'why would you want to know that,' every time I asked him a question, and when I asked for his phone number so I could give it to you, he said he never gives it to anyone, and added that he doesn't believe in letting people know where he lives. He speaks with a mountain accent, so I reckon he's local."

"Brent said he lived in Sugar Cove, something like that."

"There's a Sugar Grove just a few miles from here."

I had another icy chill. "Sugar Grove is what he said. Are you all right?"

"I'm okay. The police here know I didn't have anything to do with Johnny Shook's death, but some people are avoiding me, and I catch others looking at me like they think it's my fault that he was stalking me, and if I hadn't been here he'd still be alive."

"Do they say that?"

"No."

"Do you think it's true?"

"Of course not." Her tone was dismissive of the idea.

"Because it isn't true at all, but maybe you feel guilty anyway."

"I didn't do anything, Daddy."

"I didn't say you did. It's normal to feel guilty when somebody dies like that, and maybe you're projecting your feelings onto other people."

She laughed. "Thanks, Sigmund Rutherford."

"You are all right, aren't you?"

"Yeah, I am. How about you and Mom?"

"We're muddling through. She's got her cross and I've got mine. Let me know if this Ken Byrd calls again. Maybe you should tell the police about him."

"Why tell them?"

I had an uneasy feeling that, somehow, in some way, Kenny Byrd had something to do with Johnny Shook's murder. I still couldn't remember him, and wondered if Brent was somehow tied up with Joseph. But with the saner realization that any such conspiracy would have to include Jan, I quickly sloughed the suspicion off.

"He sounds like a whacko, and I think it'd be a good idea to let them know you're concerned about him and what he might do."

She agreed, and after reassuring one another of our love, we hung up.

By the time I reached the High Ledges, the temperature was in the low nineties, the air steamy from the storm. The small parking lot at the top of the access road was full. I parked the car along the side of Patten Road, pulling as close to the edge as I could without driving into the ditch. Several cars and pickup trucks passed as I was getting out and locking up, kicking up stones from the gravel road, and even raising some dust, in spite of the recent rain.

The head of the trail leading to the High Ledges is a garden. Ferns, primeval with their delicate ancient fronds, wildflowers, azaleas, and mountain laurel gave way to trees as I followed it down toward the preserve. Small animals watched from the shelter of their nests and dens, or peered from behind rocks and undergrowth. A fox stood still beside a blueberry bush, the quivering of his nostrils the only indication that he was a living creature. I breathed deeply of the country air, scented with pine and blossom, relishing the moment, the quiet, removed from the turmoil that had lately become my life.

Happy for a peaceful respite, a chance to let go of my worries—if only for a brief time—I wandered through the woods. I passed a group of people coming from the preserve as I hiked toward it, birders I guessed, from the cameras and binoculars they carried. We exchanged trivialities about the ferocity of the previous night's storm and the day's heat.

"Bugs are bad down there," said a tall woman with white hair in two pony tails that hung over her ears and fell to her shoulders. Older than I by at least a decade, I took her for one of the Ur-Hippies who came to Franklin County long before Haight-Ashbury entered the national consciousness, one of the type who are now living what they describe as "the simple life," financed by large trust funds they have inherited from the parents whose values they came to the country to abjure. She set down an Audubon Society canvas bag, took out a water bottle, and drank from it.

"The people suck, too," said a young man with her. He wore baggy pants, and his arms were covered with tattoos. There were studs in his nose and tongue, his blonde hair streaked with green food dye. "There's people all over the place today. Gram cussed at a couple of them that was smoking weed down by the cabin. I'd'a asked them for some, but she just cussed them, didn't you Gram?"

"They could start a fire, smoking down there like that," the tall woman said. "I don't care if they smoke a joint or two, drop acid or whatever. I don't even care if they do crack cocaine, shoot up heroin, or whatever else gets them off. God knows, my friends and I did enough drugs back in the days. What I object to is where they do it and how it can put other people and the environment at risk."

"I'd go back if I were you," said a woman wearing a Smith College t-shirt, dungarees, and heavy hiking boots. "Gram and Arnold are right. It's really quite unpleasant down there today."

A third woman, dark haired and heavy set, also wearing a Smith tee, agreed. "Between the bugs and the people and the heat, it's pretty unpleasant."

"They never should have opened the place to the public," the woman with the white pony tails said between swigs from her water bottle. "If I had known how it would turn out, I certainly would have thought twice about donating to the Society. Places like this are fragile; large groups of people just degrade them. The Society should restrict access to members only."

"You said it, Gram," the tattooed boy said. "People ruin everything." He sniffed deeply, leaned over, and spit just off the side of the trail. He looked up at me. "What happened to your eye?"

"Stop that, Arnold." His grandmother looked at me. "You just never know what they're going to say, no matter how old they get."

"He's right," I said. "People ruin everything. Look at what you folks have done to my morning."

Before she could reply, I continued down the trail toward the Ledges. The boy called "fuck you," after me, and the last I heard was his grandmother hissing his name.

Covering almost six hundred acres, the preserve can absorb a moderately large number of people and not seem crowded. I wandered the trails for a while, then left them and ducked behind a thicket of low blueberry bushes into a secluded spot to have a private picnic. I drank the first of my three beers to wash down the peanut butter sandwich. The second I drank for the sheer satisfaction of drinking a cold beer on the first stifling hot day of the summer.

The third went to an elderly man who saw me sitting against a tree several feet from the trail.

"Looks good, that beer, I don't suppose you've got another." He stepped through the bushes. His white beard neatly trimmed, he wore a dark blue suit with a pink shirt and what appeared to be a Jerry Garcia necktie. His shoes were polished black leather, scuffed and dusty. Somewhere in his late seventies to early eighties, he looked wildly out of place.

I wanted to say no, but his smile was wide, his face hopeful, and I passed my last can to him. "You're in luck."

"Thanks." He cracked the tab, raised the can to his lips, and took a long drink. Lowering it, he sighed and belched. "Sorry. Guess I drank it too fast." He spoke with the clipped Yankee accent of the region. He held out his hand. "Name's Norman Hubbard."

"Have you been out here long?" I introduced myself as I shook his hand.

"I live here."

"Here?"

Smiling, he shook his head. "Down the road, that first drive you see coming in. I still do a little farming, not much anymore, but enough that me and Edith take care of most of our food and have a bit left over for the kids as well." He pointed back toward the main entrance. "We're having a wedding, my grandson's. I got bored with the whole affair and took a walk." He looked down at himself. "Not the best woods wear, eh?"

"A little unorthodox. So you're not lost?"

"Hell no. I've been coming here for sixty years, before the Audubon folks ever heard of the place." He leaned over, looking toward the paper bag resting against my knee. "That a gun you got in there?"

"Where," I said, folding the top over.

"In your bag. Looked like the butt of a pistol sticking out, and judging from the way you were so quick to cover it up, I figure I'm right. You've got a pistol."

"It's for self-protection. I'm being stalked by a lunatic."

"Planning on killing him?"

"If I have to."

"I killed a man once. Wouldn't want to do it again."

"What happened?"

Using his foot, he cleared a spot next to me, kicking leaves and twigs to the side. Sitting down, he took another long drink from the beer. "Not worth talking about. I'd like to forget it, but a man can't let go of how terrible it feels to take a life. All I say to you is that you should think about what you're considering doing. Kill whoever it is that's after you, and you'll never be rid of him. Got a permit for the gun?"

I shook my head.

"Good. If you kill the guy, it'll make it harder for the police to pin it on you, assuming you get rid of the gun in the right way. Won't be any ballistics history they can use to trace you, no numbers to run down if they got no paperwork on it. You know how to get rid of a gun?"

"How did you get rid of the one you used?"

He looked confused, then his face cleared. "Hell, I didn't shoot the son-of-a-bitch. I strangled him. Looked right in his eyes as he died, knowing that I was killing him, and knowing why I was doing it. I been looking in those eyes ever since, wondering why I did it."

"What happened to you?"

He took a last swig, holding the can high as he emptied it. "Not much." He looked as though he was about to say more when I heard men's voices calling. "My boys," he said. "Probably come to drag me back to the wedding. Thanks for the beer, and think more than twice before you do what you're thinking about."

He slid the empty beer can toward me. "Don't let 'em see this."

I tucked it under my knee. Norman rose just as a man in his mid-fifties came through the bushes. "Hey, Pop, Reg and me have been looking all over for you." His voice was gentle and patient.

His father gave him a sly look. "You should've looked right here. Been sitting talking to this fella for a while now."

"Hope he wasn't a bother," he said, pointing to his father.

"Actually, he's been helpful."

"Been telling you stories, has he?"

"It's been an interesting conversation."

"Don't mind him. He wanders a lot, and makes up the most outlandish stories. It started when he was in his early sixties, but he's been like this for a while now. My wife says we should take him to a doctor, get him in a home or something, but he took care of Reg and me when we were kids and Ma was sick for several years. Guess we can take care of him now."

Norman straightened his back and cocked his head at his son. "I can take care of myself, thank you. Been doing it for seventy-five years, me and Edith."

"Eighty-six years, Pop."

"That's even more impressive," Norman said.

"Impressive as hell," his son said. He took his father's arm and began leading him back to the trail. "Come on, Pop, let's go. The J.P. said he'd put the wedding on hold until you were back."

Putting my trash in the bag with the pistol, I hiked around for another hour or so. The afternoon grew cloudy, looking like another storm was building. I saw fewer people as time passed, but the storm never developed, and soon the sun was shining. I found a mossy spot in a grove of oaks and maples, and lay down, intending to close my eyes for a few minutes.

It was nearly dark when I woke, the moon a crescent sliver visible through the canopy, the sound of a lone owl the only break in the quiet. I walked the trail to the overlook at the rim of the ledges, and in the early evening gloom, looked at the view of Deerfield, the lights of scattered farms and those in the village of Shelburne Falls. Standing in the still of the gathering night, I jumped to the sound of a twig snapping on the trail behind me, afraid Joseph had somehow followed me there and was approaching.

I turned, and saw a deer and her fawn standing at the tree line, staring at me with a fearful look. An instant later, they turned and darted into the woods, the mother's white tail disappearing into the forest. It was a harmless moment, but it startled me from the brief peace I had found. Joseph might not have broken the twig, but he broke into my thoughts, reasserting himself and the fears that accompanied him.

I headed back to the car. The parking lot at the head of the trail was empty. Twenty feet away, at the edge of Patten Road, my car sat alone, covered with dust. I tossed the paper bag containing the pistol on the passenger seat and drove toward Greenfield.

Jan was hungry when I got home, and neither of us had thought about dinner. I stashed the gun in the drawer of a small table in the hallway and, after calling in an order for Chinese, I went out to get it. When I returned, I saw she had she uncorked a bottle of Chianti and set a table on the front porch. We ate and drank to the sounds of rumbling trains in the East Deerfield switching yards and loud rock and roll coming from a music festival at the Franklin County Fair Grounds.

"To a lovely, peaceful evening on Tuckerman Court," she said, clinking her wine glass to mine, and we drank. A motorcycle thundered past the intersection at the foot of the street. After several sips, she put her glass down. "My epiphany isn't going to chase you away, is it?"

"Would it change anything if I said yes?"

"No. What has happened to me is irreversible."

"Let me remind you again how you used to say you could never live with someone who believed in such crap."

"That's when I believed it was crap. This is different."

I raised my eyebrows in a silent question.

"I was talking about preachers with their narrow-minded ideas about Jesus, and churches. That's still all crap."

"No doubt about that in my mind, and as for the rest of it, your epiphany or whatever, I don't want to argue. I'm not going to leave you. Maybe if this had happened when we were courting, I would have broken it off, but there's too much water over the dam at this point in our lives."

"You're such a romantic devil." Her beeper went off as she laughed and raised her glass. She looked at it. "Rats. The hospital. I should have been a psychiatrist, anesthesiologist, any specialty with regular hours."

She went inside to call the hospital, and came out carrying her bags. "Don't wait up. It could be a long night; the Anderson baby's a breech." Brushing a kiss across my lips, she left.

My wine glass was empty. I finished hers and poured it full again. I hadn't heard a car, or any footsteps, but when I looked up, Joseph stood leaning against a pillar. He was dressed in a burlap robe, and wore a crown of thorns on his head, a pair of crude sandals on his feet.

"All the sacrifices I've made for you, and you wouldn't even have breakfast with me this morning." He shook his head sadly. "But I knew you would deny me, and I forgive you."

"What in the hell do you want from me? What do you think I've got to give you?"

"Only that you shall love me as I have loved you. Surely that isn't too much to ask."

"You don't have a right to ask me for anything. I just want you to get out of my life. And why are you dressed like that?"

"I knew it would get your attention." He pushed himself away from the pillar into an upright position. "Those cops, Bourbeau and Novak, they showed you what they thought was my body. What did you think?"

"I knew it wasn't you. I saw you on the road to Williamstown after whoever that was had already been killed."

"Perhaps I was resurrected."

"Perhaps you're full of shit."

"That could be. Or you could be terribly deluded."

"You're here. Ergo, you can't somewhere else."

"Brilliant logic, Professor." He bowed. "And why am I here, do you think?"

"I don't know why you've done anything you've done since the day you and Randy beat me up and left me blind in one eye."

"About that," he said. "Lift your patch."

I refused.

"Lift it." It was not a request.

"No."

"I have ways of compelling you to take it off."

"I'm not afraid of you anymore."

"Sure you are."

I shook my head. "I'm really not."

I was telling him the truth, although I did not know how I had arrived at the point where he no longer threatened me. In retrospect, it may have a result of too many visits from him in too many guises, and too many forced conversations in which he would try to one-up me and I would try to hold my own.

"Kenny Byrd may have something to say about whether or not you're afraid."

Again, the icy stabbing chill.

"Show me," he said. "Show me that you're not afraid. Let me see your eye."

"I don't have an eye under the patch."

"Show me."

Afraid for Mimi, what the mysterious Kenny Byrd might do to her, I would have done almost anything Joseph told me to do. I took off the patch.

"That's ugly," he said, looking at the still-raw wound where my eye had once been.

"Thanks to you, asshole."

He laughed. "What a creative mouth you have, Professor. Surely someone with your education and experience can come up with a better response."

"How does 'fuck off, asshole' strike you?"

Shrugging, he reached out and touched the wound with his finger. He shook his head with an exaggerated mock seriousness, shutting his own eyes as he spoke. "I'd heal it if I could, but I'm afraid I wound people rather than heal them. It's a cross I have to bear." He pointed at the wine bottle. "I don't suppose you'd be willing to share a little of that."

I seized the opportunity. "Wait here. I'll get you a clean glass."

Inside, I got my gun, and returned to the porch, pointing it at his chest.

"Oooooh," he said, clapping his hands together in what appeared to be jubilation. "Professor Rutherford, what took you so long? Have you any idea how long I've waited for this day?"

"You want me to kill you?"

"No one wants to be killed, Thomas. At least no one in his right mind, but if killing me will save you, then I make the sacrifice willingly and lovingly."

"You want me to kill you."

"That depends on how you define the word 'want'. 'Need' might be a better word. I need you to kill me if you're going to survive and prevail."

I kept the gun aimed at his chest, unwavering. "I don't understand."

"Of course you don't. You never will. There was a time when you would have grasped all this clearly, but the time is past. All I can promise you is that this will all recede and lose importance to you."

I clicked off the safety.

"You've had the gun locked all this time," he asked.

"But no more."

He stood erect. "Do it. Shoot me."

I took a step toward him, the gun firm in my grip, aimed at the spot on his chest directly over his heart.

"Shoot," he said.

I stood still, my finger on the trigger. The gun felt cool and smooth. I looked into his eyes. They did not falter. Gripping the gun with both hands, I raised it and tightened my finger on the trigger.

"Shoot," he said again.

I looked at my watch. It was twenty after eleven. We stood facing one another, me with the gun, he silent, his eyes fixed on my good one. My breathing was regular, and I felt calmer than I had in days. I was aware of time passing slowly, but not of the time itself. We stood facing one another. I measured my breaths, inhaling, counting to ten and exhaling for fifteen seconds, then inhaling again. The next time I looked at my watch it was one minute before twelve.

"Midnight would be a good time to die," I told him.

"No time's a good time to die, Thomas. Midnight would be appropriate."

Midnight came and passed. At ten after, I lowered the gun and put the safety back on. Its clicking sound seemed louder than the noises rising from the switching yards and those falling from the Fair Grounds.

His eyes blazed, and his upper lip curled as he spoke. "You will rue this failure unto the end of your days. We are finished, Thomas. This is your final betrayal of our friendship. You have no virtue. Do not expect to see me again. Not ever."

The phone rang.

I stood still through four rings, before the answering machine turned on and I heard my voice ask the caller to leave a message. It was Bourbeau, and I half-turned away from Joseph in order to better hear his message.

"Good news, Professor Rutherford. It's your man. You're safe from him now. We do have a few questions for you, however. Please come down to the station in the morning."

He rang off, and I turned back to Joseph, the pistol hanging limply in my hand.

He was gone.

I have not seen him again, nor have I heard from him. It is as though he has vanished from the earth. But I have accepted him. He has entered my heart, slipped in like a murderer's knife, and the world is a flatter, colder place for his being there.

LaVergne, TN USA
03 May 2010
181361LV00002B/73/P